T0117106

Crime and Management,

A Novel
and Other Tall Tales

Eugene M. Silverman

iUniverse, Inc.
New York   Bloomington

Crime and Management, A Novel, and Other Tall Tales

This is a work of fiction. All of the characters, names, incidents, organizations, and dialogue in this novel are either the products of the author's imagination or are used fictitiously.

iUniverse books may be ordered through booksellers or by contacting:

iUniverse
1663 Liberty Drive
Bloomington, IN 47403
www.iuniverse.com
1-800-Authors (1-800-288-4677)

Because of the dynamic nature of the Internet, any Web addresses or links contained in this book may have changed since publication and may no longer be valid. The views expressed in this work are solely those of the author and do not necessarily reflect the views of the publisher, and the publisher hereby disclaims any responsibility for them.

ISBN: 978-1-4502-1907-5 (sc)
ISBN: 978-1-4502-1908-2 (ebk)

Printed in the United States of America

iUniverse rev. date: 3/25/2010

Dedication

To Nathan, alev ha shalom, who showed me, and to Andy, Josh, and Elliott, who continue to show me, the warmth and kindness of manhood.

To Goldie, alev ha shalom, all four feet, eleven inches and ninety six pounds of her, who showed me, and to my valorous wife Alida, to Marilyn, Leslie, Stacey, and Shirin, who continue to show me, the power and wisdom of womanhood.

"God's benison to you; and with those that would make good of bad and friends of foes." William Shakespeare, *Macbeth*, Act 2, Scene 2

"Simply by finding and reaching those few special people who hold so much social power, we can shape the course of social epidemics. In the end, Tipping Points are a reaffirmation of the potential for change and the power of intelligent action. Look at the world around you. It may seem like an immovable, implacable place. It is not. With the slightest push in just the right place it can be tipped." Malcolm Gladwell, *The Tipping Point*

Contents

Forward

Human history is littered with the bones of conquered, vanquished, subjugated, and slaughtered tribes and nations and the wreckage of their wealth and achievements.

From the earliest tribes to the largest nation states, conflict among these gang members and with neighboring gangs has wreaked havoc among us. Those of us now alive have been lucky enough to have ancestors who managed to escape this turmoil long enough to beget us.

Mostly, the leaders of these gangs have exploited their followers and wasted their blood and lives attempting to control, colonize, enslave, or exploit the neighboring gangs and steal their treasure.

The question posed by Crime and Management is whether or not we can find leaders clever and forceful enough to motivate the tribes to work together instead of against each other and in so doing minimize the violence that seems inherent in us.

Crime and Management

Chapter 1

The house was a duplex, as were all the other houses on Seventy Sixth Street between Twentieth and Twenty First Avenues, in the Bensonhurst section of Brooklyn. It had stucco walls, a concrete stoop in front, and a pair of concrete lions guarding the entrance, one on either side of the stoop. To the left of the stoop, a statue of the Virgin guarded the house and its occupants, from the middle of a small rectangular plot of earth sparsely covered by grass. Carmine and his parents lived in one half of the duplex. "Uncle" Tony and his family lived in the other.

Inside the house, Carmine snuggled on his mother's lap, his cheeks buried warm and secure, in between her large breasts. Daddy was still sleeping.

"Joseph Carmine, today is your fifth birthday and I got you a wonderful surprise. Want to unwrap it?"

"Yea, Momma, but is Daddy coming to look at it too?"

"Not right now Carmine; Daddy had to work late last night with Uncle Tony. He'll come down in a little while and show you how to drive it."

The unwrapped bright red pedal car had a padded vinyl seat which Carmine climbed onto, his feet easily reaching the pedals. He clutched the steering wheel, moved his pelvis forward, stretched out his legs, and found to his delight that he could pedal and feel the car move forward slowly over the rough pavement. Now he could go anywhere with his own car, but Momma said only on the sidewalk.

He got out and looked at his car. It had a small mirror stuck on the front, near the steering wheel. Daddy would show him what that was. It had headlights at the front and a trunk in the back. He loved the new car! *I bet my car has everything on it that Daddy's car has.*

He came back in to the house, slipped into the garage and stared at Daddy's car. It was so big! He pulled open the front door and sat in the driver's seat. His feet couldn't reach the pedals unless he held tight to the steering wheel and stood on the pedals. "I can't pedal it," he thought. "Maybe that's why you need a key, to be able to pedal it. What did all the buttons do?"

He pushed, pulled, or turned every button or knob on the dashboard. Finally, there was a pop from the rear of the car and the trunk lid opened.

Carmine got out of his father's car, went around to the back, and standing on tiptoe, peered into the trunk. Maybe there was money in it like a few days earlier when Daddy had taken Carmine on a ride to a house in the country. Daddy had taken a big package of bundled up money from the trunk and brought it to a man in that house.

Under the trunk lid was a light which now shown onto something covered by a large plastic tarpaulin. Carmine lifted the edge of the plastic closest to him. Underneath he felt a cool form. It felt like fingers. It had fingernails. It was a hand. The fingers were stiff and didn't bend. He moved to his right, and lifted the plastic. Underneath was the head of the doll, bloated and blue, with mucus and blood around the nose. Carmine began trembling and ran from the garage, into the house, and into his bedroom. He never spoke of this to anyone.

In a short while Uncle Tony came over and he and Daddy went into the garage. Daddy came out. "Marie, did Carmine go into the garage?" he asked his wife.

"I'm not sure. Why? What's the matter Joe?"

"My car's trunk is open. You didn't open it did you?"

"No, Joe. Why would I fool with your car?"

Joe ignored his wife's last question and went to Carmine's room.

"Hey, birthday boy, do you like your new car?"

"I love my new car," Carmine lied, trying to smile, and hid his trembling hands behind his back.

"Were you just in the garage?" asked Joe.

"Sure," answered Carmine, as calmly as he could, I wanted to see if my car had everything on it that your big car has."

"You didn't open the trunk, did you?"

Carmine knew the answer his father wanted and knew that he wanted to believe that Carmine had not seen what was in the trunk. At this realization, Carmine's anxiety abated and he was able to answer convincingly, "I was playing with the buttons inside the car and something made a popping sound. It could have been the trunk. I don't know. I didn't look at the trunk."

"You sure?"

"Yes Daddy, I'm sure."

His father smiled, patted him on the head, and asked if he was all right. Carmine said "Yes."

Joe kissed him and left in the car with Uncle Tony.

Chapter 2

In Bensonhurst, kids grew up early. At fifteen, Carmine ran the family's numbers business. He arranged the odds so that that the profit averaged twenty percent of the take. The percentage had to be big enough to make it worthwhile, but small enough to be competitive with other bookmakers and with the track. And, there was no tax to pay on the winnings. By sixteen, Carmine was innovative in choosing the source of the winning numbers. Those numbers, which changed daily, were always to be found somewhere in the one page business section of the New York Daily Mirror.

From early on, he stopped taking bets on credit. Carmine's focus was always on balancing profits with risk to the family. His cash-only policy resulted in fewer debts being forcibly extracted from people who got in over their heads. It also meant that people could not bet if they exhausted their capital. Threats and violence were no longer necessary. There was less violence, a lower profile, and less risk for the family.

Two years later Carmine began attending Brooklyn College, majoring in political science, with a minor in business. He especially enjoyed reading *The Prince,* written about five hundred years earlier by another Italian, Niccolo Machiavelli. It was tricky, but good to be prince!

Carmine's father expressed his pride in his accomplishments by giving Carmine his second car, this one a full size Chevy Camaro. One night he was leaving a social gathering of the younger Bensonhurst mob members and he offered three other teens a ride home. The youngest of these was Uncle Andy's nephew Louis Cannone. The three teens asked Carmine to stop at a McDonald's for burgers. They offered to get the food while Carmine waited in the car. They asked Carmine to park in the furthest spot from the store "for exercise."

In a few minutes, he heard a gunshot and saw the boys running from the store, one carrying burgers and another with a fistful of money. They pulled stockings from their heads and threw them out of the car windows a few blocks later as Carmine sped away. Andy's nephew, Louis replaced a small pistol in his jacket pocket.

"I had to shoot the bastard." He whined, "He was goin' to come after me with a knife."

"You prick!" yelled another of the teens, "He was gonna' give you the money. He was just putting the plastic knife and fork in the bag with the burgers. "You shot him just to see what would happen to him. I think you only got him in the hand, thank God."

Carmine shook with fear and rage at Louis, and horror that the kid at McDonald's had been shot. He had participated in the shooting by driving the getaway car. He suddenly was overcome by nausea. He grabbed the bag with the burgers, emptied it on the floor of the car, turned away from the other boys, and vomited into the bag.

What could he do? He couldn't report the robbery to the police. These were young members of the Bensonhurst gang, his father's people, his people. Briefly, he considered turning them in. But surely the cops wouldn't believe he didn't want to be involved. But involved he was. And turning the other boys in wouldn't do a thing for the kid who had been shot.

Carmine was tormented. He dropped the three others at Louis' house and drove home. He followed the reports of the robbery in the Daily Mirror. The cashier was a sixteen year old boy who played the clarinet in his high school band. He had been shot in the hand and two of his fingers were mangled and had to be amputated. Carmine decided to confront his father with his problem and the two of them worked out a prescient solution. His father, Joe arranged to have some money deposited in an anonymous annuity account which would pay the young boy enough to carry him through college and a few years beyond.

Carmine thrived on his success at managing the finances of the gang but was tormented by the thought of the violence it created. His thoughts more and more focused on how to reduce the violence and reduce risk it caused to his organization and to everyone else.

By Carmine's twenty first birth day, his father, Joe, was head of the Bensonhurst branch of the Brooklyn Family and Carmine was indeed a prince. His skill lay in modernizing the family's investments so that they were not only profitable but also garnered support for the Family from various important parts of the community. Carmine's Cacciaguida Financial Service storefronts began to appear and multiply across the city. These businesses managed investments for ordinary people. Financially trained staff managed portfolios arranged so that they were age appropriate and diversified according to asset groups with different proportions in stocks and in fixed investments. CFS soon formed a group of their own mutual funds. They hired the brightest analysts to purchase and manage stock portfolios for these mutual funds and these funds did well.

One of the most profitable of these funds was CSF (Cacciaguida Select Fund), composed of shares of various Family ventures. Schoolteachers, shopkeepers, police, firemen and politicians became part owners of these ventures by owning shares of CSF. A majority of the voting shares of this fund was owned by the

Family, which was always in control. But lots of people had a stake in the well being of these businesses.

The fund had no trouble being profitable; it was just a matter of deciding how much of their income would be reported by the businesses. There was always plenty of income for dividends to shareholders and for charitable endeavors. The fund was a steady contributor to the Church, and to other religious groups, and to the Police Acknowledgement Association. The PAA would use this donation to provide a monthly cash gift to one meritorious police officer from each precinct in the city. There were no uniform standards as to how the recipients were selected and the gifts were usually rotated among all the officers in a precinct.

Now, what better place could there be for betting on the numbers, Carmine reasoned, than the Cacciaguida Financial Services storefronts? These offices were popular with everyone, including the police.

Carmine's organizational skills did not go unnoticed, especially by his father Joe.

"Carmine, you make me a proud father. One day, I would like for you to take over for me. But, there's one thing you gotta do before anybody in the family is gonna trust you or respect you. I'll wait awhile to tell you what it is."

For Carmine, it was enough that his father had chosen him. He could wait to find out what he needed to do.

Chapter 3

Bulova Johnny's Time is Up

It was a cold evening in February several years later that Carmine learned what he had to do. He was on a snow-covered fire escape, climbing up the steel ladders to just outside the living room of "Bulova" Johnny's apartment. He was shivering and sweating at the same time, partly from the cold, and partly at the thought of having to kill Johnny. He didn't know what Johnny had done to merit the hit and he didn't ask. It was time to take this final step required to earn the trust of the Family.

Uncle Tony had said, "Carmine, you gotta do this. You think good and people like you but you ain't **in** 'til after you spill some brains on the floor. So that's why I'm aksing **you** to do this."

The fire escape was in the alley, facing the brick wall of the next building. A light flickered on the second floor. Carmine flattened himself against the wall. The shade on Johnny's window was pulled half way down. Carmine crouched and peered through the lower half of the window. The walls of the room were covered with clocks old and new, tall clocks that stood on the floor, small hanging clocks, and all sizes in between. A wooden worktable was littered with clock and watch mechanisms, some assembled, and some not. Carmine could see Johnny's hands over the table, prying the face off a turn-of-the century mechanism but he didn't have a good view of the rest of Johnny.

Carmine waited. In five minutes, as his friend Andy and he had planned, the doorbell rang. Johnny picked up a pistol from the table and walked to the hallway, just out of sight. Carmine reached into his coat pocket and fumbled for his handgun. He managed clumsily to get the gun out of his pocket. When he looked up, Johnny and Andy were in the living room. A surprised and angry Johnny was staring out the window at Carmine. Johnny raised his pistol and pointed it at Carmine's head. Carmine was holding his gun but his hand was weak. He couldn't pull the trigger. He heard a shot but nothing hurt. Johnny fell forward, blood gushing from the back of his head. Andy's gun was smoking. Andy opened the window for Carmine, who climbed in. They both left by the stairs.

"Don't worry Carmine," he said, "as far as the rest the family is concerned, you killed him. What really happened here is our secret." Carmine was on his way upwards in the "family."

"Andy, why would you do this for me?"

"Because you are my friend and because the Family needs you."

When Papa Joe died, Carmine inherited the leadership of his Bensonhurst organization.

Chapter 4

Ten years later, Andy sat at a table for two, waiting for Carmine. He looked like his father, Carmine's now deceased "Uncle" Tony, with thinning gray hair. He was portly and showed every one of his forty two years. He wore a camel's hair sweater, buttoned half way up the front, partly covering a white shirt, and a black and bronze patterned tie, which, if looked at with a magnifying glass, would appear much like a Mauritz Escher picture. But the intertwined images would be blackjacks and brass knuckles. To the unaided eye, however, these subtle details were not evident. Andy had a sense of humor, but liked to keep a low profile. He ruminated:

"Lunch with Carmine at Papa Leone's- not bad. Something important. I wonder what he's thinking up now? Thinking is what he's good at, thinking and bullshitting. Better at bullshitting than doing. Yet people listen to him. So it's high quality bullshit. Still, way back from the fourth grade on through high school, there was a reason I always sat next to him when there was a test. Same reason why he's padrone. Good friend, good boss, good place, Papa Leone's. Tina may call the office, wonder why I'm not there, think I'm with my wife, Shit! Where's Carmine? Here he comes."

Carmine arrived, his tan, handsome still youthful face, smiling at the sight of his old friend. He was five foot, ten inches in his slightly built up shoes, a small concession to his own battle between life-long modesty and increasing vanity. He was no longer at his college weight, but was still trim. His hand-made blue pinstriped suit and light blue Versace shirt were topped off with a lavender and blue striped necktie.

"Carmine, cetriole (cucumber), Che si dice?"

"Sto bene, I'm fine, salsice (sausage). Thanks for coming out to Manhattan to meet me. You're my oldest friend and I value your opinion. I want to bounce an idea off you to see what you think."

Andy replied, "This must be earth shaking or crazy if you dragged me all the way to Manhattan, so go ahead and bounce."

"It's both. How would you like to get paid for sitting on your ass - no jobs to pull, no gun, no knives?"

"I'd feel naked."

"No cops, no chance of jail time?"

"No shit? You're kidding right?"

"No shit. If we can pull this off, we get paid for not doing crime. It's something I've been mulling over for some time and I think I have enough of the bugs worked out, to see if I can get support for it from the people who could make it happen.'

"Just what are they gonna make happen?"

"I call it Managed Crime."

"Managed Crime? That's where we don't do nothing and get paid for it?"

"Almost. It's where insurance companies collect money from the government, and employers, and people, to insure them against being victims of crime. If they get mugged, they get reimbursed. But there won't be much crime."

"Why not?"

"Because we and the other major players will get paid by the insurance companies every month not to do crime, and, if crime happens, the victims get paid out of the money we'd have gotten from the insurance companies. So if money is stolen, it'll be deducted from our monthly payment and be used to pay the victims. So there'll be no reason to pull off any jobs."

"So let me see if I've got this right. We're gonna tell Rudolfo Malocchio in Staten Island, who likes to carve up people for the fun of it, and dissolve them in acid, that he should be a nice guy, go to church, and say "excuse me" when he belches. And, we should ask him if he could please not grind up his enemies and feed them to his pet Dobermans? Right Carmine, that's all we have to do?"

"Look Andy, if we can convince the more reasonable bosses that this is a workable and profitable scheme, those who don't come in on the deal would cost the rest of us money, which we would not tolerate. Also, there'd be some solo operators and small groups with which we'll have to deal. Some, maybe, we let join; others we have to crush. That'll give Malocchio and Tanner something to do to keep in shape. There are nine other major New York groups so we'll have lots of convincing to do."

"What do you mean **we**? **You** have a lot of convincing to do and you might as well start by convincing **me**!"

The waiter silently approached the table. "Would you like to order something to drink? We have a nice Valpolicello."

"How about we split a bottle of Chianti, Carmine?"

"OK by me. Bring us a bottle and I'll have a Caesar salad."

"Bring me a linguine a la mezzogiorno."

"So, you want me to give up a nice, profitable job as your right hand man to go into the insurance business with you? I've got to think of my family. There's my wife, my son who's going to go to medical school, and my girlfriend Tina, and her apartment?"

"Andy, let's start with the potential market. There are nine million or so people in New York City. If each one paid a modest fee, say five dollars a month for this insurance, that comes to forty million dollars a month, or four hundred eighty million dollars a year to go around. People pay fifty times as much for health insurance. So, conservatively, we can expect at least fifteen dollars a month, which amounts to one billion four hundred forty million dollars a year to split up. And that's just the beginning."

"So who's gonna pay us all of that dough for just doing nothing?"

"Insurance companies. And who's gonna' pay the insurance companies? It'll be like health insurance. People will pay and the companies they work for will offer it as a benefit. For poor people, the government will pay just like in Medicaid, and for old people, the government will pay just like in Medicare."

"I still don't get it."

"Andy, this is really nothing new. It's probably the oldest racket."

"Prostitution?"

"No, protection. It's just a marketing thing. We're giving it a new name for the twenty first century. Does it make sense now?"

"Carmine, protection I understand, but this idea bugs me. On the other hand, I've been with you since we were kids, and if you think this will really work, I'm interested."

"Andy, we're years away from anything to be in. For now, it's just an idea and there will be lots to do before it can be anything more, but I really like this idea and I'm going to go for it with everything I've got."

"Gentlemen," the waiter had again silently appeared, "Signor Milocchio, the owner of this place, wishes to thank you for honoring his restaurant with a visit, and hopes your meal was satisfactory. He sends his kindest regards and insists that the meal is complimentary."

"What a nice surprise. I had no idea that this was Rudolfo's place. Please thank him for us and tell him Carmine and Andy are in his debt."

"It is not Rudolfo, but his son Isidoro who is the proprietor, and he would be delighted to join you for a moment if that is agreeable to you."

"Please tell Isidoro that we would like for him to join us and to congratulate him on his acceptance to Yale Law School."

J. Isidoro Milocchio, the twenty three year old son Rudolfo Malocchio, head of the mafia family in Staten Island, was tall, thin, and conservatively well dressed. He was handsome and could model suits for the most expensive lines of men's clothing. Isidoro was poised, comfortable within and with others, and had the relaxed, easy going manner that put other, lesser folk at ease. His long face was graced by a perfect nose, altered only slightly, as was his surname - from Malocchio (evil eye) to Milocchio (a thousand eyes.) His fingernails were carefully manicured.

"Mr. Cacciaguida, Mr. Buonocore, a pleasure to renew old acquaintances" he told the two men. "The last time we met, I believe, was at my confirmation many years ago."

Carmine was impressed by this handsome young man. "Congratulations on your success at Yale. Now we expect you to keep your Papa Rudolfo out of trouble."

"No, Papa Rudolfo is keeping me out of trouble by buying this restaurant for me to run until school starts. There is so much to learn. The mayor came for a visit last week and Senator Strong was here last month, I get to meet distinguished guests, as I'm now doing and, occasionally get to overhear interesting bits of conversation."

Only then did Andy notice the small vase of flowers on their table but not on any others. *Was that small metal wire holding the flowers a tiny microphone? Had Carmine been out-foxed by Milocchio? Or had Carmine come here deliberately to let Rudolfo know about his idea?*

Chapter 5

A few Years from Now

Joseph Carmine Cacciaguida was now the most successful crime boss ever in New York City and people could walk the streets without fear.

Today, as Carmine strolled through Central Park with no bodyguards, he thought of his father, Joseph, who usually had at least one bodyguard. He thought of Carmine Desapio, the source of his middle name, who was the brilliant and corrupt last boss of Tammany Hall. Carmine's surname, Cacciaguida meant "hunter's guide" in Italian. An interesting name, he fancied, for a personal ad he'd thought of running after his wife, Bernice, died eighteen years ago. "Mob boss likes Gershwin and cozy walks in the park with my (at the time) bodyguards. Want the prettiest 30 year old woman I can buy who will love me for myself." Not surprisingly, he never placed the ad.

He paused to pick up a large red ball and handed it to the mother of the child who had kicked it in Carmine's direction. She smiled and thanked him.

When his idea for managed crime was new, it was hard work getting support for it from the people he needed. Finally, he got that help in an unlikely place.

Carmine had adjusted his tie and dialed the phone. "Mayor LaGuardia, this is Carmine Cacciaguida, one of your great fans in Brooklyn. I have an idea that could benefit the good citizens of our city, save the city some money, and help your administration become as revered as that of your great uncle Fiorello."

"Really?" said the woman's voice at the other end of the line.

"And you won't have to read the funnies on the radio to the kids to do it."

Fiorella LaGuardia looked at the caller ID and smiled wryly, adjusted her dark hair, and answered. "Carmine, my great uncle Fiorello is revered because his administration put crooks like you in jail and didn't make deals with them."

Carmine laughed gently. They had never met, but Carmine suspected from her response, that things might go well. "I like your candor." He said "You'll make a great ally when you catch on that we're both on the same side."

"Not a bad opening. Original," she thought. But she said, "I see, so you want to rat out all your friends, put 'em in jail, and become an altar boy?"

Carmine couldn't help smiling, "Not quite, but maybe we could get them to stop committing crimes and even help to prevent crime. Would that be a step in the right direction?"

"Carmine, come to the office next Tuesday evening and we'll talk. I want you to look me in the eye and tell me all about this idea. I need to be looking at you when you fill me in on what must for sure be a bunch of sugar-coated bullshit."

"I'll be there and I'm not bullshitting you or trying to bribe you. But I will make you an offer you won't want to refuse."

Fiorella LaGuardia was perplexed by Carmine's call, and also wondered if she needed a new outfit for Tuesday.

The Mayor's office was quiet in the evenings and the mayor was alone on Tuesday night when she ushered Carmine in and offered him the seat across from hers. Fifi, as she enjoyed being called, inherited her famous great uncle Fiorello's short stature, fiery temper, and sense of humor. Her pretty, middle-aged face resembled that of her great grandmother, Irene Luzzato Cohen, Fiorello's mother. It might also have been from Irene Cohen that she had inherited her taste for bagels and lox.

"Your honor," purred Carmine.

"Cut the shit, Carmine," growled Fiorella, "If you're on the level, you can call me Fifi. Otherwise, get the fuck out of here."

Taken back by her gruffness, Carmine cajoled her, "OK. Fifi. If you'll listen to what I've got to say, call me Carmine. Otherwise I will get the fuck out of here."

"I **am** calling you Carmine! So, I'm all ears."

Carmine looked around the office. On the wall behind her desk, were photos of Fifi's family. In the center was one of her late husband, a fighter pilot who died ten years ago in the Middle East. They had no children. To the left, was a picture of her parents, both short and stout. *"Like teapots,"* thought Carmine. To the right was the famous photo of her great uncle Fiorello La Guardia, seated behind a bank of microphones during newspaper truckers' strike of nineteen forty five. Fiorello read and embellished on the newspaper funny pages to the kids of New York who listened on the radio.

Fifi cleared her throat. "So, you were going to tell me how we're gonna save the City?"

Carmine turned from the photos, wondering how much Fifi resembled her crusading great uncle who spent his life fighting corruption. She sounded tough, but she was willing to listen. "The idea, simply stated, is that managed crime works like an HMO, only it's for crime."

She shifted in her chair and bent slightly leaning towards him, "So you're selling me insurance?" she said firmly, "I come in to the office in the evening for you to sell me insurance!"

"She sounds tough, but why is she showing me a little bosom?" thought Carmine. "I'm selling you the **idea** of insurance. The idea is that in managed crime there would be insurance companies that collect money every month, from people or from businesses that offer it as a benefit to their employees. The federal government

would have plans like Crimicare for old people, and Crimicaid for poor people, to help them pay their share of the insurance."

Fifi's tone softened a bit. "You're talking insurance against crime?"

"Exactly! Now, here's the good part. In HMOs, the health care provider groups guarantee to take care of their members' health for a set amount per month. They don't get paid for each service. If everybody stays healthy they don't have much to do and they get paid anyway. Managed Crime works the same way. The Crime Management Organizations, CMOs for short, will be insurance companies that sign up groups of criminals and pay them money every month *not* to do crime. In fact, for any crime that happens, the victims are reimbursed for whatever money they lose, for pain and suffering, medical costs, and lost wages, and the insurance companies take that amount of money out of the pool that would otherwise go to the criminals."

Fifi was now interested. She reached into a desk drawer, pulled out a box of Ghirardelli chocolates, offered one to Carmine, and nibbled away at another. "So Carmine, what you're saying is that all crime that happens, instead of being good for the crooks, costs them money whether or not they're the ones who committed the crime?"

Carmine reminded himself to bring chocolates to their next meeting. He was sure there would be one. He swallowed the melting chocolate and continued. "That's right Fifi, it means the criminals have no incentive to do crime and every reason to make sure that nobody else does either. Now, Joe Crook on the street can't guarantee anything. Just like an individual doctor can't guarantee to provide complete health care. It would take a large, powerful group of organized criminals who are responsible for most of the criminal activities in any region to decide to get paid by CMOs to stop doing crime and to help prevent anybody else from doing crime. That's where the Network comes in."

The feisty Fiorella returned, "So, with managed crime, suddenly all of your, would you call them 'colleagues', switch sides, become vegetarians, take off their black hats, put on white ones, and suck on lemons all day?"

Carmine thought for a moment. "Right," he replied, "except for the lemons. There would be some serious and maybe dangerous work to get the other, I'll call them "non-network providers of criminal services" to join us in the managed crime business." It was warm in the office and Carmine felt the sweat forming on his brow. Do you mind if I take off my suit jacket, Fifi?"

She shook her head. Carmine removed the jacket and added, "And by the way, just like with HMOs, where some health care services are covered and others are not, with CMOs all violent or potentially violent crime is covered except for distribution of illegal hard drugs and for terrorism, both of which involve international cartels that we couldn't yet control locally."

Fifi's eyes widened as she began to realize that Carmine's plan would involve her. "So you're here because you want to start all this in New York City? Are you patz (crazy) in the head? How on earth do you think you could do it?"

"We'll need the proper legislation locally and nationally to allow for Managed Crime to exist and to partially finance it."

"So how are you going to do that? Where are you going to start?"

"I think I might have some luck with Payne Strong. Then I'll contact the governor, and key members of the state legislature to see if they would like to reduce spending by reducing the costs of crime to all of us. There would be savings in the costs of incarcerating criminals, requirements for police services and costs of overburdened courts, not to mention the benefits to business of safe streets."

Fifi suddenly felt, that she had him. "That's great. So we convince all these folks that managed crime is the answer to all of our civic problems. But how do we get the crooks to go along with this terrific plan?"

Now it was time for Carmine's checkmate. "Madam Mayor, with even some evidence that there is support from New York

City's administration, and a hint that the City might start it off by enrolling its employees in such a plan, I can guarantee you that we could get all of the eleven major crime families in the city into a network that could control much of its violent crime. That would be my job. In short, there'd be no benefit to Network members to actually commit crime and there would be every incentive to eliminate crime by its members and by others."

Fifi stood, offered Carmine her hand and signaled the end of the interview. "Carmine, you've got a good line of BS. Let's see what you can do."

Chapter 6

Payne Strong was in the fourth year of his second term as senior United States Senator from New York State. It was Monday evening and he was home watching the Jets play the newest expansion team in the NFL, the Mexico City Federales. Carmine's package had arrived by courier. The message left by Carmine on Payne's private home answering machine was intriguing. Carmine had asked for a meeting between them the next day, at two PM, and to expect a pleasant package. Payne would give up his golf game tomorrow to see what his biggest campaign financial supporter had in mind. Page opened the package and it contained a large pair of sunglasses and a jacket with elastic bands at the ends of the sleeves, and with "Pipefitters Local 23" on the back. "Joe" was written in script on the front, over the right breast. A small note in the package read "Meet you at the Brooklyn Botanic Garden at the Magnolia Plaza. Please wear these."

Payne appreciated that his acquaintance with Carmine, and even more, Carmine's financial support of his political efforts, was not common knowledge. Carmine also seemed to enjoy going about in public without being recognized. Payne didn't usually mind being recognized, but not with Carmine.

The Brooklyn Botanic Garden, adjacent to Prospect Park in the center of Brooklyn, was a marvel in the spring and summer, with more than twelve thousand different kinds of plants, including the Bonsai Museum, the oldest and largest collection of dwarf trees in the U. S. There was also a garden for the blind, with brightly scented and textured plants, and the Magnolia Plaza, adorned with seventeen varieties of these elegant trees. In the Spring, throngs of visitors abounded enjoying the glorious scent of these trees, but now, in the fall, there would be few visitors to this spot and Carmine and Payne could expect to go unnoticed.

Carmine wore a grey jacket with "Jets" lettered on the back and "Charlie" on the front. He was waiting at the Magnolia Plaza when Payne arrived. They were alone. Carmine began ebulliently to describe his plans for managed crime and the network that he would create. Payne was wary but warmed to the idea when Carmine mentioned that Mayor LaGuardia had promised (Carmine stretched the truth here,) to implement the plan in New York City if the appropriate federal and state legislation were passed to legalize it.

"Well," said Payne, "what happens to the income from the Cacciaguida Select funds if you guys give up on all of your lucrative activities?"

"There'll still be plenty of activity left to make lots of money for your grandchildren's college funds. I can also guarantee a sizeable contribution to your next election campaign."

Payne said he would think about how an enabling bill could be written and submitted simultaneously in the Senate and the House. He was thinking about the downside of sponsoring such a bill but didn't mention these thoughts to Carmine. How would it look for him to be openly allied to organized crime? And, what if Managed Crime was merely a rip-off of the general public and would be expensive and ineffective? *Taking a personal active role on this venture could be a career-ending move. What to do?*

"Carmine, I'm not sure I want to have a high profile on this adventure. How would you feel if I convinced another senator to sponsor the bill?"

"That's OK, as long as it has your full support and you do all you can to get it passed."

"We need to talk a little more about the details of your campaign contribution," said Payne, and after a long pause, "and possibly a little about the funds we would need to hire lobbyists for the bill, but it's worth considering."

Carmine walked with Payne to Washington Avenue where a limo waited for Payne. The driver opened the door and Payne climbed in. Carmine reentered the Garden and strode eastward toward the Japanese Hill and Pond Garden on his way to Eastern Parkway where he could get a cab. In the pond, the day-blooming water lilies were white and pink and in full bloom and the deep red flowers of the night bloomers were sheathed in their outer green leaves. Several varieties of lotus plants were resplendent with yellow, red, or rosy pink flowers.

Movement on the edge of the pond caught Carmine's attention and he noticed a mature painted turtle struggling out of the swampy water, onto the grassy slope, to bask in the sun. "Way to go turtle!" he thought.

Carmine was less encouraged by his discussion with U.S. Congressman Enoch Carter, an African American who had grown up in Harlem, gone to Columbia University, studied political science at Cambridge on a Fulbright scholarship, and then earned a Doctor of Divinity degree from Harvard.

They were seated in Dr. Carter's office in a storefront building in Harlem. Class photos of students taken at a small charter school that Carter had started in Harlem hung on the walls of the office.

Reverend Carter sat in a comfortable but worn arm chair across from Carmine. He believed in good and evil and in personal responsibility for one's actions, good or bad, and he had no use for Managed Crime.

"Mr. Cacciaguida, how are we going to get rid of crime by institutionalizing it, by rewarding criminals, and by teaching kids that the way to get ahead is to join a gang?

We need to help them build character, to know right from wrong, to take responsibility for their families, and to encourage them to become useful people with skills that will contribute to and be rewarded by others. We need to emphasize education and to have schools that will keep the kids in them until they graduate."

"We need to increase head start programs. We need safe schools with enough books, supplies, and computers and with enough good teachers to staff them. I don't see how Managed Crime will be of any use here in New York City."

Carmine was impressed by this man's sincerity and replied. "Those are lofty goals, but meanwhile, while we're working to improve the schools, we could save lots of lives by reducing violence and providing gainful, honest, work for lots of youngsters in the Network's management and counseling services. Also, I suspect that we could easily work out an arrangement to contribute part of our revenue to help improve the City's schools."

"Mr. Cacciaguida, I would prefer to raise young people who could become professionals, and leaders in business, politics, religion, and the arts and sciences. I have nothing against you personally, but I think that you and I can never agree on this issue. I will not support Managed Crime now or ever."

"Reverend Carter, I respect your opinion and I can sympathize with your point of view. But I believe strongly that Managed Crime has the potential to reduce violence in this state and in others while we wait for the next generation and I'll work tirelessly to make it happen. When Managed Crime happens, and it will happen, I'll look forward to working with you and other principled people who didn't at first agree with me."

Carmine was told by his advisers, that they could surely delve into Carter's history and find useful tidbits to discredit him but Carmine was sincere about eventually convincing this intelligent and good man to work with him as an ally and arranged for a personal contribution to Carter's school's scholarship fund.

Chapter 7

Arch Jones sat behind a worn but functional wooden desk in the Raeburn House Office Building. It was evening, the sun had set, and through the window, only the lights of Washington DC were visible. Framed diplomas from Rutgers University and Fordham Law School, and a portrait of Arch and his family hung on the wall behind him. In the photo, his five children, were seated in front of their smiling parents. Certificates of appreciation from the NAACP, Hadassah, and Catholic War Veterans of America flanked the diplomas and family portrait.

On the far wall was a large photograph of Arch in the Oval Office, shaking hands with the president of the United States.

At the moment however, in his office, Arch was unclothed as were Veronica and Elizabeth who were perched, respectively above him on a bar stool, and below him on a cushion on the floor. The phone on the desk rang plaintively but was ignored by the trio. Moments later, Arch's mobile phone rang and got a different response. Arch gently removed Veronica's nipple from his mouth and answered the ringing phone.

"Carmine? Hey, I do appreciate your generous contributions to my campaign fund, especially since I'm a Republican. Yes, Strong and Her Honor the mayor already called me."

He reached down and removed his wilting member from Betty's grasp but stroked her hair. Continuing his conversation with Carmine, "Yes, Andy from Brooklyn and Gardner from Newark left messages for me. I see. So even the criminals, no offense meant, are going to go along with this idea of yours. I've already told Strong that I like the idea. I guess he called me because I'm on the House Subcommittee on Crime, Terrorism, and Homeland Security. I'm pretty sure I can get someone from the other side of the aisle to cosponsor it with me. Veronica and Elizabeth are terrific. Best temporary office help I've had in a long time. Great heads on those two! Thank Mila for sending them all the way from Brooklyn. No. I'm not worried about my wife finding out about the girls. You wouldn't be subtly threatening me would you? Not necessary. I actually like your idea! I'm on board."

(A short while later)

A statement from the honorable junior senator from New Jersey, in the Senate Proceedings, (and a similar one from Arch Jones in the House Proceedings) said. "Under the proposed Managed Crime Act, criminals, after providing sufficient evidence demonstrating appropriate experience in various criminal activities, are registered as providers.

Citizens, being potential recipients of criminal activities, are enrolled as members, either individually or through plans sponsored by their employers, with the assistance of the federally sponsored Crimicare program and the state and federal governments'-sponsored Crimicaid programs. Payments are made, per member per month, by Crimicare, Crimicaid, individual citizens or their employers, to local, regional, or national insurance companies called Managed Crime Organizations. These MCOs contract with the criminal providers, usually in regional groups or networks, to prevent violent or potentially violent criminal activities. All ordinary crime with the potential of violence is disallowed under the plan, and costs of any actual crime committed are deducted from the payments that the network receives. In addition, the network of providers is put at risk for any crime committed by non-network criminals so that the cost of such crime is also subtracted from network income. Networks will use any lawful means to discourage criminal activities by themselves or others in their regions. Where these efforts are not successful, they will assist the police in using lawful methods to deter further violent criminal activities by those so engaged."

The federal Managed Crime Act (with riders endorsing appropriate pet projects of several senators from small states, and potentates in the House,) was passed by the House and Senate. Soon after, similar legislative packages were passed in the legislatures of New York State and New Jersey, which enabled and partly financed Managed Crime in those states.

Chapter 8

It was an ordinary day, shortly after the Managed Crime Act had been put into practice. Valerie, a young woman teller said "Hello" to and smiled at the elderly security guard as she made her way into the Dime Bank of Brooklyn. "That" she thought, "would make this retired policeman's day." She hurried past the other tellers, to her seat behind the counter. She was a little late this morning as she had dropped off her two toddlers at the day care center and made her way through traffic on Eighty Sixth Street to the bank. She had just enough time to brush strands of her dark brown hair from her face, straighten her cardigan sweater, and sit down in her place before the bank opened its doors for business.

Valerie's first customer was a middle aged woman resident of the nearby Marlboro low rent housing development. The woman was waiting at the door when it was unlocked and hurried to Valerie's window with her saving account book in one hand and a withdrawal slip in the other. The withdrawal was for five hundred dollars again. The last time she had withdrawn five hundred dollars was when she had confided, her teenage daughter had gotten pregnant and needed an abortion. Valerie wondered what sort of emergency it could be this time. She handed the woman five one hundred dollar bills, smiling at the worried looking woman who took the money quickly, said "Thank you" and hurried away.

Her next customer was a burly man wearing a white T-shirt, blue jeans, and sunglasses. He handed her a note, but before she could read it, she heard a commotion from just inside the bank's entrance where she saw the security guard fall to the ground. Blood streamed from a knife wound to his groin. A man with sunglasses stood over the guard holding a knife. Valerie, now terrified, looked at the man in front of her who was now pointing a revolver at her chest. He handed her a cloth sack and pointed to the note, which said. "Push the alarm and I'll blow your head off. Fill this with lots of tens and twenties and no dye."

Valerie opened her cash drawer and removed the bundle of bills with the concealed dye pack, and several other bundles, and put them into the sack. As she handed them to the robber, he pulled the trigger, saying "Bitch, I told you no dye packs." He left the sack on the counter, followed the other robber out of the bank, stepped into an old red Chevy Caprice and disappeared, leaving the guard dead and Valerie on the floor, and the staff at the day care center waiting in vain for Valerie to return to pick up her kids.

Chapter 9

Harlan's new office at the FBI was on the twelfth floor of the Manhattan Federal Building at Twenty Six Federal Plaza and his name, Harlan Dreyfus, was stenciled on the door. There was a not too comfortable swivel chair to keep him awake, and an unobstructed view of One Hundred Eleven Worth St., a dull eighteen story building across the street, just right for minimizing the distraction of the New York City skyline which would otherwise have been visible just beyond.

It was time to unpack books, some still in their book covers with Stanford Law, in bright red letters, and others with Brown University emblazoned on them. One book from his undergraduate days, a text from Professor Buckwits' economics class, rekindled memories of an old ember, Claire Cacciaguida; (it takes two to for a flame and this relationship was strictly one sided.) He would sit a row behind her and a few seats to her side to avoid her noticing his staring at her. She was petite, with her dark hair held in a bun with two large wooden hairpins. She was olive skinned, soft voiced, and determined to understand it all, especially when it came to health care policy. She was certainly a beauty, even more appealing with her large, aquiline nose.

On a chain around her neck, was the biggest cross he had ever noticed on a woman. Maybe it looked so big to him because he was Jewish or, could she be a nun? Whatever the reason, this cross was big enough to be used as a weapon if she ran out of Mace. The Mace was in a small canister on the key ring she kept in her purse, which once she had emptied onto her desk in search of her eye-glasses, also disgorging a lipstick, tissues, a one hundred dollar bill, and a packet of birth control pills. So much for the nun idea. He guessed that after Brown, with her interest in health care policy, she would go on to medical school but instead she had gone to Harvard Law School. He'd heard she'd got herself a master's degree in public health as well as a law degree. Go figure!

The ring of the telephone interrupted these reveries and brought Harlan to the harsh reality of a voice. "Dreyfus? Harlan?"

"Yes.'

"This is Bill Cleaver, your alter ego, sometimes mentor, biggest critic, slave driver, and the one who will fire your ass if you screw up, so get it over here to my office so I can brief you on what you'll be doing here."

Chapter 10

With her degree in Public Health, working out the basics of managed crime had been a no brainer for Carmine's daughter Claire. She used managed health care as her model. HMOs are insurance companies who figure out the cost of health care and then calculate the average monthly cost for each insured person. Then they line up Hospitals and doctors and offer to pay them a little bit less than they can charge people to be insured. Most people get the insurance as a benefit of being employed or through the government via Medicare and Medicaid.

To decide on the cost of insurance coverage for crime, Claire determined the average cost of each type of crime to the victims. She added medical costs, lost wages, and a factor for suffering. Then she added the sums of total costs of police, the criminal courts, and incarceration. Using the proper mathematical models and actuarial data on the frequencies of each major type of violent crime, she calculated the average cost of crime per citizen per month. This was tedious work but it laid the groundwork for figuring the charges needed from each insured person and for probable necessary government subsidies. And finally, Claire had fed it all to Papa Carmine over time so he believed it was his idea. And, after all, she did love her Dad and he deserved lots of credit for getting the idea into the hands of the right politicians, organizing the Network and helping to convince both houses of

Congress to pass bills that would end up as the Managed Crime Act, the first major innovation in reducing violent crime since jails were invented.

Naturally, when Carmine was elected president of the network, he asked Claire to manage it, smart man that he was.

The Network had thrived. Word was, there was even a new FBI agent assigned to watch over it. Harlan Dreyfus. Sounded familiar to Claire. Could it be the guy from Buckwits' class, the one who was always staring at her, the one with the big nose? Him, an FBI agent? She wouldn't have thought so.

Then she went back to work on the agenda and the Manager's Report for the next monthly Network meeting.

Chapter 11

Tuesday, October fourteenth, with no rain forecast, was a perfect opportunity for a ride to Limber's place in the new Volt 2, the quietest, greenest, most beautiful car Carmine had ever owned, and his first convertible ever. In fact, it was his first recent car without the armor plating. After all, he was now totally legal and seemed to have no living enemies. Why would he have enemies? Everybody was doing fine. Criminals, cops, courts, and jails had it easy and the citizens could safely walk the streets. Almost safely anyway, since violent crime had been down an average of thirty four percent since the Managed Crime Act was implemented last year, and was down another four percent in the first quarter of its second year.

He enjoyed the sight of the Volt's broad rounded rear, smooth sides, and gently bulging front fenders. He slid his hand over the round rump and slipped into the driver's seat, all leather and wood trim, turned on the electronic control module, waited two seconds, and glided off smoothly and quietly as only the driver of an electric vehicle could, and enjoyed the wind on his face.

Finally, the stylists in Detroit had matched the beauty of their cars with an electronic propulsion system that eliminated the need for engine cooling systems, ignition distribution systems, and gearboxes. The new Volt 2 had fantastic acceleration, and could go for eighty miles without having to resort to its small biodiesel engine to charge the batteries.

The trip from his place in the Trump Towers on Central Park West and Sixtieth Street to Limber's in the Dakota on Eighth Avenue and Seventy Second Street, was a pleasant ten minute drive in good weather and light traffic.

Limber buzzed him in. In jeans and a sweater, she combined the virginal clean-cut sweetness of the girl next door with the sensuousness of a girl in a Victoria's Secret catalog. Actually, Carmine found her on page thirty seven of last year's November issue of that catalog. With a few well placed phone calls, Carmine had ordered her. She had arrived, along with the nightie and so far, all had worked out well.

The apartment was warm and there was incense burning. She kissed him and put her arm in his.

"Hello, Carmine honey, your daughter called."

He put his arm around her slender model's waist. "Claire called? What did she want?"

"She calls me 'Mom.' She's twenty nine. That makes her two years older than me."

Carmine chuckled and entered the apartment, dropped his suit jacket on a large upholstered chair, and stroked Limber's neck. "Cute. But why did she call?"

Limber gently caressed his forehead. "She said she needed to brief you before tomorrow's Network meeting."

Carmine drew nearer to her, and loosened his tie. "Thanks. I'll call her back tomorrow morning. How's your headache?"

Limber mused "What headache?"

Carmine winked at her, "No headache? Good." And they moved to the bedroom.

Later that evening, Carmine and Limber relaxed in their seats at the Met as the orchestra played the overture. The opera Turandot had a dated and silly plot but the music was glorious as one might expect at the Met, and the final lyrics of the tenor aria

"Nessun Dorma" stayed with Carmine as he and Limber headed back to the apartment.

"Al alba vincero. Vincero! Vincero!"

("At dawn, I will be victorious! Victorious! Victorious!)

Chapter 12

Harlan's boss William Cleaver, had a bigger office than Harlan's, with a better view. Across Lafayette Street, Cleaver could see the City Hall Building, with the names Ramazzini, Hippocrates, Paracelsus, Pinel, and Lind, visible in a horizontal line on the Duane Street side, and Harvey, Billings, Ehrlich, and Leeuwenhoek on the Lafayette Street side. Harlan wondered about the haggling that must have occurred to keep all of New York City's ethnic groups represented.

Cleaver's office was not much better furnished than Harlan's and the carpet was equally worn. Bill Cleaver was in his early sixties, tall, slightly paunchy, with facial features that suggested he must have once been handsome. He had no visible hairline or part, but otherwise his hairpiece was hardly noticeable. His greeting was warm. He put his arm around Harlan and ushered him in.

"Good to see you again, Harlan. Welcome. With most of us on antiterrorism and the rest on drug trafficking, you'll be pretty much alone on the issue of managed crime."

"Good to be here, sir. Should be pretty interesting, keeping track of the crooks who are now supposed to be the good guys."

Cleaver grinned. "Call me Bill, and 'supposed to be' is the issue. These are not nice guys. They'll behave only as long as it's in their interest to do so." He winced. "Some will be working the system both ways: they'll get the revenue from the insurance companies and still do particularly lucrative crimes. And then, there'll always be rivalries." He pulled a package of Juicy Fruit from his desk drawer, offered Harlan a slice, and continued. "As you know, white collar crime and corporate fraud aren't covered by the Managed Crime Act. So you'll only have to worry about violent or potentially violent crimes. It's also clear that managed crime has only been effective against crime originating in this country. Check with the Managed Crime Financing Administration for the latest figures. They're the agency that disburses U.S. government funds for managed crime and they also collect data on all reported criminal activity."

"We do too, don't we, with the FBI Uniform Crime Reporting Statistics?" Harlan questioned.

Chewing heavily on the Juicy Fruit, Cleaver replied, "Yea, but MCFA breaks down the types of crime into much finer detail so they can get a better handle on costs and reimbursements."

Harlan shifted in his chair. "So far, crime is down but there have to be glitches in the system. I personally never buy a system in its first production year."

Cleaver laughed gently, walked to the window and gazed out briefly. "You're right. We haven't made much headway against terrorism and against imported drugs. So far, the Network has refused to cover these areas in their contract. They say they aren't ready. They don't have control of them. But Cacciaguida is willing to look into whether they can do so in the future. So we'll still need to keep those activities separate from managed crime for the moment."

"*Cacciaguida*," Harlan thought, "*that's a familiar name. Wonder if he's related to Claire?*"

The cafeteria in the federal building was a Wendy's. Harlan nodded to a cheerful looking man with a Classic Double burger and a handlebar mustache seated alone at a table for four. "Mind if I join you?"

The mustached man nodded assent. His ID badge identified him as W. Wax, FBI.

"Is your first name, Wayne?" Harlan asked, having seen "Wayne Wax" on the door adjacent to his.

"Yea. You the new agent? Managed crime?"

.Harlan sat down opposite to Wayne. "Harlan Dreyfus. Nice to meet you."

"The niceness wears off. I seem to irritate people." Wayne Wax slurped on the straw protruding from his melting Frostie. "Actually, I'm glad you're here. Cleaver had me looking after managed crime part time along with my other work until you got here. I was assigned to Carmine Cacciaguida. Quite a strategist!"

Wayne Wax bit into the burger and an orange tan mixture of mayo and ketchup squirted onto his handlebar.

Dreyfus suppressed a smile. "The more I hear about Cacciaguida, the more interesting he sounds."

Wayne tongued the flavorful ketchup-mayo off his mustache. "Absolutely! He actually got to testify before House and Senate committees explaining how and why it all would work, and to meet with the president before he signed the bill into law. Almost stood with the president, the majority leader, and House whip during the signing but that got squelched for PR reasons."

"Wonder how long Wayne has been here?" thought Harlan. *"Seems enthusiastic. Will I still find this job interesting in a few years?"*

"But," he wondered out loud, "Cacciaguida can't be all that perfect. After all, he is a long time Mafioso. Must have some interesting history in his past?"

"Not much. Rumors of a killing way back, but I do have something more interesting to give you. Come visit me later this afternoon and I'll give you the 'Hiro' file. Hiroaki Nishiyama is a cop who came to see me last week with some interesting thoughts about a recent bank robbery in Brooklyn".

Chapter 13

Claire, Carmine's daughter, was in her living room on her stationary bicycle and churning at a steady clip watching the rain splatter the dirt around the bluebell plants in her window box. A Bluetooth headset was hanging from her right ear while her left hand adjusted the pedal pressure upwards. "Carmine, I hope I didn't wake you. You're not the early bird you once were since you bought Limber. Not getting enough sleep?"

Carmine, still in bed in his apartment, laughed. He shifted upward in the bed. "All right Claire, let your papa have some fun in his dotage."

Claire pedaled faster. "You can have plenty of fun at the Network meeting tomorrow afternoon. By the way, I saw you at the Met last night. Iz and I went after work. He has a box. I think he's got a thing for you. He spent as much time staring down at you as he did at Turandot. Even when we screw, I wonder if he's more interested in you than in me."

Carmine feigned surprise. "Screw! Well, Isidoro Milocchio's certainly got a future, but I didn't think it would be as my son in law."

Claire reached for a bottle of water and squirted some into her mouth. "Not so fast with the son in law. Right now, I'm not sure if you'll get a son in law, daughter in law, or some furry little other species of mammal. I'm sure it will be a mammal, but otherwise, don't get your hopes up."

Carmine sat up and put on his brown felt slippers. "At least he has good taste in women, and in operas."

"He left singing the last few bars of your favorite aria, the one that ends in "Vincero! Vincero!"

"And in arias. So what's on the agenda for tomorrow's meeting?"

Claire checked her heart rate on her wristband monitor. "Financials for the first quarter, I'll present them. Then we can shake them up with some more interesting developments. I can tell them about our negotiations with Rock of Gibraltar, the latest insurance company to want to form a managed crime organization." Claire grunted and lowered the difficulty setting on the bike a notch. "Iz and I are using the capitation rates from our contracts with other CMOs, especially Blue Star/Blue Defender and Olympus as a starting point and things are going well. Gibraltar expects to have one hundred fifty thousand covered lives in six months. That, times sixteen dollars per member per month comes to almost twenty-nine million dollars per year in additional revenue for the Network."

Carmine was now out of bed and heading for the coffee maker in the kitchen. "Great. That shouldn't take much extra work and will help raise the ante for some of our colleagues, who always ask when our incomes will reach what we made in the old days, when we were doing crime instead of controlling it."

"It's good we'll make more because the next item is not such good news."

"Is it about leakage? That's our biggest problem. The CMOs charge us for every theft, mugging, and break-in by every two-bit punk in the city. It comes right out of what they pay us, and also, keeps us plenty busy trying to lean on those punks to stop them."

"Nice speech, Carmine," Claire said, sounding mildly irritated at this interruption. "Now would you like me to tell you what happened?" and, not waiting for an answer, "This was no two-bit punk operation. It happened yesterday, a very professional holdup of the biggest bank in Brooklyn, the Dime Bank. And worse, it was the second bank robbery in Brooklyn in the last two months, and worst of all, it was on Uncle Andy's turf again."

Carmine took a sip of the decaffeinated coffee in his cup. "Bad news. Things may get hot for Andy if the others begin thinking he's double dipping, collecting the capitation and still pulling off jobs, which comes out of all of our pockets. We'll have to deal with this situation tomorrow afternoon."

"And, we'll have to mention your interview with Katie Kewtie on Prime Time AM."

Chapter 14

Wayne Wax's office was a carbon copy of Harlan's except for the photo on the wall of the Brooklyn Dodgers, circa nineteen fifty seven, the last year the Dodgers played in Brooklyn.

Wayne was distracted by his wife's unhappiness with how little time he had to spend with their daughter Lisa. Last evening, she had scolded him for working late and missing Lisa's middle school volley ball game. He put this problem out of his head and asked Harlan, "You a Dodger fan?"

"Not since they left Brooklyn for L.A. I've never gotten over it. Pro sports no longer interest me. It's all about money.

"It's always been about money," Wayne said, "Some of us figured that out long ago. When I was a kid, I had a friend who hoped the Dodgers wouldn't win the pennant and play the Yankees. He was a Yankee fan and hoped they would play another team with a bigger stadium so they would make more money. I thought he was nuts but he was just ahead of his time. Soon, we'll get to the point where on-base percentages, earned run averages, and runs batted in will all be measured in terms of salary so we will all know which players give the best value for the buck."

The sight of his wife's sad face when Wayne returned home after missing the game still haunted him. So he returned to the topic of sports, always his escape from worries. "For basketball players, where a little notoriety helps sell tickets, to judge a player's value, they'll figure points per game divided by salary, multiplied by the percentage of the body covered with tattoos, and the number of arrests divided by convictions."

Harlan asked, "Talking about arrests and convictions, what information did you want to give me?"

Wayne shifted in his seat. "Hiroaki Nishiyama, a Brooklyn cop from the sixty seventh precinct. Hiro came to see me last week. Wouldn't talk on the phone, wouldn't meet me at his precinct, or at my office. We met at the Stage Deli. He had corned beef and cabbage; I had pastrami on rye. He was concerned that this was the second recent robbery of the same bank. In this one they used a Chevy Caprice. Andy Buonocore's gang used to use Chevy Caprices, only this one wasn't stolen."

Harlan was intrigued at this detail.

Wayne continued, "It was registered to Bidetto Passalacqua, one of Andy Buonocore's men. But Bidetto disappeared months ago and Buonocore claims not to have seen him since."

"Strange," Harlan wondered, "to use a car registered in your own name in a bank robbery,"

"Hiro said the same thing. He also told me that in Andy's gang's jobs, the notes they passed to the tellers were typed. This one had a note made up of words clipped from a newspaper and pasted to the paper. Also, nobody got hurt in those old jobs. In this last job, it was almost as if the perps wanted publicity. They killed the young woman teller and knifed a guard in the groin. Hiro seemed really pissed off. I asked him how far they got investigating this last case?"

"Nowhere," Hiro said, "just like in the last robbery at the Dime a few weeks ago, the lieutenant was satisfied that this was on Buonocore's turf, and reported it for stats and for victim reimbursement. He wasn't interested in any more work on either of these cases," Hiro added, "and that was that. Managed crime or no managed crime, these recent holdups were peculiar and I thought we should have done more checking. I called your office at the FBI because I didn't trust the lieutenant. There's still no interest in doing any serious looking into it. I offered to take the case but they gave the case to another detective who did nothing."

Wayne added, "By the way, Harlan, we checked and the words on the note were clipped from the Wall Street Journal. High-class hoods. There was a note like this one two years ago at a bank in Staten Island. Never caught the perps in that case either."

Chapter 15

Wednesday morning was always Claire's morning to herself. First it was to the gym, and then to Bloomingdale's.

The walk from her Sutton Place townhouse on Fifty Ninth Street and Second Avenue to the gym was a short one. She took the flight of stairs two at a time up to the gym on the second floor.

She removed her ipod from her locker, strapped it to her arm, put on her earphones, and moved to the track.

The oval track was one twentieth of a mile around. Claire usually did three miles of combined walking, jogging, and running. She stepped onto the track and began to jog, trying to keep pace with to the uneven tempo of the Merry Widow Waltz. It wasn't easy. She noticed a young, handsome male trainer working with a thin dark haired young woman. He put small boxing gloves on her hands and mitts on his own hands. At Claire's next turn around the track, she could see that the trainer was encouraging the young woman to punch the mitts. On the next lap, the woman was tentatively jabbing at the trainer's mitts with her gloves, but barely touching them.

Claire brushed a few strands of hair off her forehead and thought "What a wimp!"

A fast-paced piece of music had replaced the waltz and Claire increased the pace of her jog. Her eyes were again attracted to the young woman with the gloves, now grinning from ear to ear and punching hard at the pads on her trainer's hands. Sweat emerged on the woman's forehead as she pounded and grunted with each blow, laughing and happily embarrassed.

"*Ata woman!*" Claire thought.

"*Another short walk from the gym to Bloomie's,*" she *reflected.* "*Push fourth floor on the elevator. Lingerie. Havana Nights. Sexy. Who would have thought ten years ago that Havana would be **in**, fashionable, glamour, night life, sexy underwear? Harry Potsky, renamed Raphe Latour, that's who, with his newest brand, Havana Ghila. And Cuba, it's our new biggest ally in Central America. All it took was Fidel's incapacity and then his death. First his brother, then his nephew, Pedro Castro ('Castro Convertible' in the Wall Street Journal,) took over. Pedro privatized everything, brought back gambling, casinos, prostitution, corruption, and all is OK again. Business was good. The Cuban economy was booming. Cuban cigars were legal. Everybody was happy.*"

"*Oh my God! Who's that looking over a black lace teddy? Is that Harlan Dreyfus?*"

He was a little older and a bit more dapper than she remembered. He definitely looked better in a business suit than he looked at Brown. "Harlan, is that you? What are you doing with that teddy? It looks a little small for you."

He feigned embarrassment, "I'm holding on to it for the time when I get lucky and find a girlfriend like you who would do justice to it."

She couldn't resist another small tease. "Are all FBI agents into teddies now?"

"Well, you do come here almost every Wednesday morning. It's as good a place as any to run into you."

"*Well,*" she thought, "*he is after all, an FBI agent.*" "So now we've met. Is this business or pleasure?" she asked.

"A little bit of both."

Claire smiled coyly, "That kind of answer isn't going to get you far in the pleasure department. You'll have to do better. Besides, I'm seeing someone."

"I don't mind a little competition, especially when it's over a beautiful girl I've admired for a long time." Harlan responded.

"*The wretch was ready for that one,*" she thought, but said, "That's getting a little better. So you **were** staring at me way back at Brown?"

"Fraid so, besides, I think that as far as the **business** is concerned, we are both on the same side of the fence, and I think we could help each other. First off, I admire your father. If I were into prayer, I would pray for him every night."

She thought, "*If Carmine was into prayer, he would probably thank you.*"

Harlan paid for the teddy and turned back towards Claire with a serious look. "Carmine seems to be doing more to control crime than anyone else on the planet. A big part of my job is to see that he stays alive. I'm not so sure about the rest of his cronies."

"I'm happy that you admire Carmine. His interview with Katie Kewtie will be on Prime Time AM next Tuesday." she bragged.

Dreyfus looked pleased, "I'll make sure to watch," he smiled, "and, since we're all on the same side here, any chance you could get me an ex-officio seat on the Network board?"

This guy had more nerve than the kid Claire knew in college. "You're kind of cute," she said, "but not that cute. It's nice to know you feel that cuddly about the Board. I'll tell them that at the next meeting. Hand over that teddy, I kind of like it. Then we can go for brunch at Zabar's Deli. My car is waiting downstairs."

Dee was waiting at the curb, in the Jaguar. Harlan was impressed by this short, young, brown-skinned attractive woman wearing a shirt and trousers, who extended her hand to him.

"Harlan, this is Dee. She's my personal assistant, bodyguard, driver, and friend, otherwise known as Durgayoni Ramalingam. Dee, this is Harlan Dreyfus. He's with the FBI. He's spying on me so I thought I would invite him over and find out what he wants to know and why. Maybe we can make life easier for us both."

Dee looked Harlan over and apparently approved. "Nice to meet you Mr.Dreyfus." She said in Indian-accented English, "This one's not so bad to look at, Claire"

"Durgayoni?" asked Dreyfus, "That's quite a name."

"I'm from South India, Mr. Dreyfus, and that name got me in plenty of trouble. My surname, Ramalingam, means 'the Lord Rama's penis.' I wanted my parents to change my first name to Megawati but they said Megawati was too powerful a name and not appropriate for a woman. So I changed it to Durgayoni. Among Hindus, Durga is the most powerful goddess and yoni is the feminine counterpart of lingam. So I had to leave India. Not much a feminist could do there at the time."

Claire opened the door of the car and gently pushed Harlan into the back seat. She got into the front passenger side, "Dee, please take us back to the apartment. Harlan, time flies and we have lots to talk about. We can have sandwiches at the apartment. How often do I get a chance to reminisce with an old Brown classmate? Besides, I want to try on my new teddy."

Chapter 16

Claire's breasts were small under the teddy and her erect nipples stared out at Harlan. Her neck curved as she bent to pull the two long hairpins from her head and allowed her dark hair to gently fall to her shoulders. She put the hairpins on the nightstand and motioned to him to move closer to where she sat on the bed. Her hands slowly undid the knot of his tie and slid the tie off. Harlan undid a shirt button and she undid the next. Her hands moved to his belt buckle and opened it. Slowly, she undid the zipper of his pants and smiled as she felt the rigid member underneath. He wriggled to allow his pants to fall to the floor. He reached for the teddy to loosen it but she signaled him to wait. She drew him down on the bed and, still sitting, removed his undershirt. She motioned to him to pull down his shorts and let fall the straps of the teddy, revealing her pink breasts moving gently as she breathed. She put his hands on either side of the teddy and he bent to pull it down, kissing her navel as he went.

They lay naked on the bed side by side. Harlan leaned towards her and kissed her closed eyes, her open mouth, her throat, and her sternum, in between her breasts, which he held in his cupped hands. She rose, and facing him, straddled him, and pressed against him, gently guiding him into her. He felt her warm wetness around him. Their rhythm was guided by her brief moments of holding her breath and her groans until she gasped, and, after a few moments, lay still. Harlan was elated and could no longer hold back the climax that overcame him.

"So, did I do OK compared to my competition?" he asked?

"It was wonderful, but why didn't you take off your shoes and socks?"

He looked down to check, "I guess they're still on then?"

She shrugged, "I guess that whatever I don't take off you stays on you."

He pouted, "Does that mean you won't marry me?"

"Harlan," Claire teased, "You're a terrific lover but it's a little early to consider marriage, especially since you're in the FBI, I work for a network of criminals, we hardly know each other and I don't know whom I would want to marry or if I ever will want to get married." Claire pulled the sheet over her, covering herself to just above her breasts, "Besides, having good sex and being married are probably not possible in the long term, with the same partner."

Harlan lifted his body and leaned on his elbow to see her from a little farther away. She was out of focus being so close to him. He was unsettled by her last comment. "That's pretty grim. How could you come to that conclusion at your tender age?"

"In my case, it's probably true. I've been pretty confused about my attachments but things seem to be sorting themselves out. My first experience was with a potted begonia, so I thought I was a hortisexual." She continued teasing and unsettling Harlan. "My next try was with a cucumber, so I thought I was at most, a vegisexual. Then there was my college roommate, Claudia. So I thought I might be a lesbian. Next, I seduced my first priest." She paused, to let him wonder just how many priests there had been. "After the second priest, I knew I was not a lesbian but wondered if I could be a gerontophile. I felt guilty about getting them to break their vows but, after a few more men and an occasional furry creature, at last I knew what I was. I am an omnisexual."

Harlan took a moment to assimilate what he had just heard. "I'm impressed, but how did you do it with Claudia?"

Now she had him, "Harlan, I just told you that I had sex with a potted plant, a cucumber, two elderly priests, and assorted furry animals. All you can ask is how I did it with Claudia? Men!"

Chapter 17

The Jaguar purred along on the way to Teterboro Airport, where Claire kept her old Cessna 150. Small planes are not permitted to fly over Manhattan and Teterboro, New Jersey has the closest suitable airport for them to take off and land without interfering with large commercial planes going and coming from New York City's three major airports.

Claire knew that Dee was not fond of flying. She looked over at Dee and teasingly inquired, "Sure you don't want to come for a spin?"

"No thanks Claire. I get enough kicks from driving this Jaguar. My parents would be amazed if they could see me driving it, and even more amazed to learn that Jaguar was now owned by an Indian company."

They drove in silence for a few miles and Dee asked, "I haven't heard much about Iz Milocchio lately. How's your new friend the good looking FBI man? Any chance for a romance there?"

"I don't think so, Dee. He's really into me. I slept with him once, and he proposed. I need someone who's more of a challenge. Iz is detached but not right either."

"So, they're either too interested or not interested enough? And maybe too young or too old? Maybe they're just not Carmine?"

"Well, Mom died when I was ten, and my grandma was around for less than two years afterwards. From then on, it was just me and Carmine. He was pretty busy and I wasn't a boy. He never said he was disappointed in me but I knew in my heart that we would have been closer if I were a man."

"I know the feeling. In my country, there was no doubt that girls were less valued than boys. I'm still working on getting my kid sister to come over here and go to college."

"I never found," Claire mused, "any man other than Carmine, that I really cared about.

Claire checked the old Cessna and sampled the gas in the wing to make sure the plane was gassed up before entering it. She carefully went through the safety routine and then started the engine. Slowly the plane moved forward and she soon felt the excitement that always came as it rose gently off the ground.

Claire rose to three thousand feet from where she had a good view of Staten Island, and then of The Statue of Liberty and then Ellis Island, through which her grandparents had entered the United States long ago.

But this was more than a sightseeing trip. She knew her old Cessna 150 was a stable craft. When she was a student, her instructor had said that "the 150 was so stable, that if it stalled, all the pilot had to do was to let go of the controls, and the plane would right itself."

Today, Claire decided to see for herself. She took the Cessna to a safe altitude of five thousand feet, set the throttle to idle, and pulled back on the yolk pointing the plane skyward. The 150's airspeed slowed. Soon the stall horn blared and suddenly the Cessna flipped over. The windshield in front of her no longer showed blue sky above. All Claire could see in front of her was brown earth and it was spinning. She was in a stall/spin and was heading straight down towards the ground almost a mile below. She had been expecting a stall but not a spin. Her excitement quickly turned to panic. She pulled back the throttle and the plane became quiet. What to do next? She wasn't sure. Could she trust the plane to correct itself?

She resisted the impulse to control the plane, took her hands off the yolk and her feet off the rudder pedals, and forced herself to fold her arms across her chest.

It took a few seemingly long seconds for the plane to stop spinning and for the airplane to come out of the stall. The windshield again filled with blue sky and she was again in control of the plane.

Back on the ground, Dee was reading a novel and was unaware of Claire's adventure. Claire didn't let on that anything unusual had happened.

"Have a good time up there in the sky while we earth bound mortals are solving the terrestrial problems of the world"

"Right Dee, the sky is still blue. But what earthbound problems are you solving?"

"Still haven't solved my own earthly quandary of what to do with my life. Working with you in managed crime has been the most interesting job I've had. Still I wonder about the future. I suspect that as an activist, I would have more opportunity here in the U.S. but there is so much more that needs changing back home in India."

Chapter 18

The Network offices were in the Freedom Tower on the site of the new World Trade Center. It took Carmine thirty eight minutes to drive there from the Trump Towers, park the Volt, and take the elevator to the eighty sixth floor. The meeting room and its central oval table were large enough to seat Carmine, the eleven other members of the Network, and Claire, the Network manager. Carmine's seat was in the middle, facing the large window. Claire sat to his left with Andy to her left. Iz Milocchio, the vice president of the Network and chair of its finance committee, sat to Carmine's right. Since Rudolfo's untimely death three years earlier, Iz had taken over his father's turf on Staten Island, and was expanding his operations into Greenwich Village, in Manhattan. Iz did very well since he collected his share of the managed crime revenue and still enjoyed income from drug sales that were excluded from the managed crime contracts. Iz was five feet, ten inches tall, handsome, expensively dressed, and self-assured as one might expect after graduating with honors from Yale undergraduate and Law schools. His only known personal relationship was the sometimes one with Claire.

The other network members were seated, like disciples around Carmine's table.

Next to Iz sat Pepe Duvallier, a Haitian who controlled the Flatbush section of Brooklyn.

Next sat Nathaniel Barth, a forty six year old African American whose turf was lower Manhattan except for Greenwich Village. He also lived in the Dakota Apartment Building.

The others, from the other boroughs of New York City as well as Long Island, Westchester County, and Newark, New Jersey, occupied the other seats around the table.

Carmine pulled his chair gently towards the table and looked from one member to another, "Before I give the president's report, I want to remind you that only topics directly related to Network business will be discussed here." He smiled and added, "I also want to mention that I will be interviewed on Prime Time AM by Katie Kewtie next Tuesday at ten AM. I hope you'll all watch. It's a good chance for some positive exposure for us."

There were smiles and snorts from the members as Carmine continued, "Now, for the president's report: All three of my topics today relate to leakage which is coming right out of our profits."

He frowned. "First, we have to deal with Hans Bruder and his sister Greta in Yorkville. We end up getting charged for every pizza sub shop and liquor store they shake down. We need to find some way to incorporate them into the Network or put them out of business. I'm appointing a subcommittee of Iz Milocchio from the Village and Nat Barth from lower Manhattan. Iz, would you head up the subcommittee?"

Milocchio: "I'll be happy to do so but I'm not optimistic that we'll find common ground with that bunch. They're small enough for us to crush if we can't come to an understanding. If you call Bruder to let him know what we've decided, I'll call him to set up a meeting. I'll let you know how it goes at next month's meeting."

Carmine nodded "Ok" and continued, "Next, we have to look at the second robbery at the Dime Bank of Brooklyn. Andy, that's your catchment area. This second one was not only expensive, but got us all sorts of bad publicity. A young woman teller got shot and a security guard got knifed in the groin. Made all the papers.

Not going to help us get new members. So Andy, what are your thoughts on these robberies?"

Andy, veins prominent in his forehead, stared at Carmine, then at Milocchio. "First off, these guys used a Chevy Caprice, which we liked for our old bank jobs. Also, the note to the teller was made out of letters cut from newspapers, which was what we used in our last job years ago. But, they haven't made a Chevy Caprice in over twenty years. These guys went to a lot of trouble to make it look like I'm involved in this. I swear on the memory of my sainted mother-in-law that I had nothing to do with either of these jobs."

Nat Barth, whose eyes had been closed, seemed to awaken, "Wait a minute Andy, how come you're swearing on your motha-in-law? You hated the bitch!"

Andy's face reddened, "Right, so why **not** swear on her?"

Nat, skeptically, "Well, two big jobs on your turf. Doesn't look good for you. Better make sure you ain't double dipping. Either that or you can't control your turf. Either way, it doesn't look good for you."

Andy, remained calm and replied, "I know I didn't have nothing to do with those heists and I know that somebody went to a lot of trouble to make it look like I did. How do we know that's not you, Nat?"

Carmine, sensing trouble, needed to change the topic. He quickly said, "Wait a minute! We've got to keep working together to make this network go. How about not jumping to any conclusions about these jobs until we learn more about them? Meanwhile, our next issue is also about leakage, the leakage that costs us money every time some idiot beats up his wife or kids. So far we don't have any control over these types of crimes but their cost is taken out of our revenues. I've been looking into this and there are programs at City College in counseling in what is now called Intimate Partner Violence. It might be cost effective to hire and train counselors who could work with families to help control this leakage."

Jaime Poquito, from upper Manhattan asked in mock surprise, "You mean like hire social workers? Old man Malocchio would turn over in his grave!"

Andy, retorted, "What grave? You can't turn over in concrete."

Claire hadn't spoken in a while and shouted over the laughter, to get their attention, "Here's an item that I think will interest you all. The network got charged back for costs associated with the beating of a thirty three year-old man, Crimicaid number 510858, in the Bronx. Total chargeback to the network for this beating including medical bills, lost wages, loss of consort, and pain and suffering have been adjudicated at one hundred thirty six thousand dollars. This subscriber showed the reimbursement committee evidence of wounds to his face, arms, legs, and anus, his medical bills, and lost time from work. The reason for my bringing this particular case to your attention is the location of the assault, which was the two hundred twenty first precinct of the NYPD. The guys who beat him were four police officers. Any comments?"

The member from Westchester County, incredulous, "So you're telling us that we have to pay all of that money to reimburse some idiot who got beat up by the cops?"

Claire, reassuringly, "Looks like it. We weren't smart enough to exclude crimes perpetrated by the cops in our first contract with the insurance companies. You can bet that problem will be fixed when we renegotiate our contract at renewal time."

Another member: "Leave it to the cops to fuck everything up!"

Chapter 19

At a small meeting room in the FBI offices, Bill Cleaver, Wayne Wax, and Harlan Dreyfus stared intently at a video screen which displayed the Network meeting room and its occupants.

Cleaver: "Which one is Jaime?"

Wax: "Jaime Poquito, the young Hispanic across the table from Carmine, only twenty nine years old, but head of a mostly Puerto Rican mob in upper Manhattan. Smart. Graduated from the Bronx High School of Science. He specialized in car theft and insurance fraud. Seems to have cut that out for now. But we're not sure. They never mention their extra-curricular doings at Network meetings. Carmine sees to that."

Harlan: "Carmine seems to be doing a pretty good job of keeping the activities of the Network itself clean. I accidentally on purpose ran into Claire in Bloomingdale's yesterday. She's Carmine's daughter, the young pretty one sitting next to Carmine. I know her from college and I think she'll arrange for me to meet with Carmine. They already knew I was assigned to watch the Network so there's no reason not to talk to Carmine if he agrees to it."

Cleaver: "OK, but don't get too chummy with Claire or Carmine! That wouldn't be professional." (Looking at the screen), "Who's the black guy who was worried about the bank job and Buonocore?"

Harlan: "That's Nat Barth, lower Manhattan, into extortion and drugs."

Wax: "Barth doesn't act like a team player to me. I'm not sure he's really into this Network thing."

(On the screen) Carmine: "Claire, what's next on the agenda?"

Claire: "Yesterday, I had the pleasure of meeting Harlan Dreyfus, the FBI agent assigned to our Network. We had a pleasant chat and he seemed to be a fan of Carmine and the Network. He believes we're on the same side in controlling crime. He said it might be easier and less stressful to meet and talk rather than spy on each other. Seemed a little naïve to me, and here's a good one. He even suggested that in order to keep in really close touch, he be given an ex-officio seat on the Network board of directors. He could, for instance, sit between Mila, and Peter."

All: "Shit!" "Shee eet!" "Merde!" "Marda" "Gamoto,"

"Mila" asked Claire, "What do you think of this guy?"

Mila, a corpulent woman with a Russia accent, responded. "Dreyfus sounds like a nice Jewish boy. Tell him to come over to Brighton Beach for a knish some time. I have four daughters."

Carmine: "OK, Claire, I'll meet with him. We might as well make use of an opportunity to work with another government agency. But we don't want to get all that chummy do we?"

(Back at the FBI)

Cleaver: "Who's the middle aged woman with the Knishes?"

Harlan: "Mila Grynzpan, the boss of the Brighton Beach area in Brooklyn. According to her immigration papers, she's forty eight years old. She began as a tax collector in the former Soviet Union. She made her living helping the Russian Mafia evade taxes. Her looks, as you can see, didn't help her prospects for marriage, but she evaded spinsterhood with a family-arranged marriage with Yuri Grynzpan. Yuri was a minor mob functionary whose job was to shake down foreign corporations that wanted to do business in the new Russia. A few years ago, he got orders from the Russian mob to leave Russia for Brighton Beach, a long time Eastern European Jewish area of Brooklyn That area is again thriving with new Russian immigrants."

Harlan continued, "Momma Cohen's Knish factory made and sold knishes on the ground floor. Yuri imported Eastern European women for the top floors. Most of the women were not told that they would be sex workers and their passports were kept 'for safety' by Yuri so they couldn't leave. All went well until Yuri suddenly found religion. One day he found himself in a synagogue, repentant and yearning for faith. He began serious study of Torah, abandoning the business to his wife Mila. Mila, as wives of orthodox Jews were expected to do, took over the family business along with caring for their four daughters and their home while her husband studied Torah. Her main interest was in her kids and simplifying her life. She was an early supporter of Carmine and the Network. As soon as she could, she gave the working girls back their passports improved their pay, and allowed those who wanted to leave to do so. Those were all offered room and board in another building until they could adjust and find other employment. Although there was considerable turnover in staff, Mila seemed to be running a successful and more democratic brothel."

Suddenly, although the network members were still conversing animatedly, their voices in the FBI room stopped and were replaced by a woman's voice with musical accompaniment.

Cleaver: "What in hell's going on?"

Wax: "Cecelia Bartoli, singing Kaddish."

Cleaver: "Who, singing what?"

Wax: "Cecelia Bartoli is an Italian mezzo soprano, and she's singing the Jewish prayer for the dead. I recognize the recording. I have the CD."

Harlan: "I think this may be for my benefit. Claire has a real shit-eating grin on her face."

Cleaver: "They must have found a way to use the music to neutralize our sound bug. Must be the modern counterpart of the old crooked politicians who had a radio playing during meetings in case they were being secretly recorded. For the next meeting, who can we get that can read lips off the screen?

Chapter 20

The Network meeting continued.

Claire: "Let's hear the report on the identity chips. With enrollment at ten percent of possible covered lives and crime down thirty four percent, lots of uncovered people are getting a free ride. In order to help enrollment, Pepe's been looking into chips that get implanted under the skin and emit short distance radio signals that identify people as covered members of an MCO. These chips will give the users a sense of security since criminals will be able to identify them and leave them alone. Our goal is to enroll upwards of eighty five percent of citizens who are eligible and these chips could help. Pepe studied these devices. Pepe, what do you say?"

Pepe Duvallier was a diminutive, tan-skinned Haitian, who had immigrated to Brooklyn eight years earlier. From driving an un-licensed taxi, to organizing a ring of illegal taxis, to ferrying prostitutes in the taxis, Pepe was doing OK. He needed to do well to support his wife and kids in Haiti, and his other wife and family in Brooklyn.

Pepe was, at the moment, consumed with worry about his Haitian wife, Jasmine, who had called, pleading with him to allow her and their two children to visit him in New York City. His Haitian family lived in the Petion-Ville area, the wealthiest region of the otherwise impoverished city of Port au Prince. "It's been almost eight months since you came back and stayed a few

64

days with us," she had said. "I miss you. Our kids miss you. My con misses you. I know you're too busy to come here. But I can come to New York with the kids. Why not, Cherie?"

Pepe felt guilty and agreed that she could come and visit him in three weeks.

Claire was now gently tapping on the tabletop waiting for Pepe's response. A gentle poke from Nat brought Pepe's attention back to the Network meeting. "Chips," he remembered, "yes chips for identifying people have been available now for more than ten years. The newer ones are the size of a grain of rice and can store all sorts of identifying information including blood type and medical diagnoses. When combined with satellite technology, they can be used to locate kidnap victims or lost pets. They're practically painless to insert."

Claire was happy to have Pepe's mind back in the room with them. "Thanks Pepe. We'll raise this issue with our two biggest MCOs, Blue Star/Blue Defender and Olympus."

Pepe, always cost conscious, fidgeted: "Will there also be costs associated with convincing the members to use them?"

"Costs will be modest," Claire replied. "We may need to air an infomercial or two."

Andy, with a glint in his eyes, "What's a nymphomercial? I'd watch that."

Pepe: "Merde a la puissance treize! Andy, will you please get a hearing aid?"

Chapter 21

It had taken a few bucks, but Pepe now had an apartment in the Ansonia Apartment Hotel on Broadway between Seventy third and Seventy Fourth Street in Manhattan. This would do nicely to keep Jasmine far from his house and his American wife and their three children in Brooklyn. If the Ansonia was good enough for Iz Milocchio, it would be good enough for Jasmine, even if she was not going to be there long.

He thought, as he sat on the bare floor of this new apartment, how he would like some help furnishing it before Jasmine arrived. It would need to look lived-in. Maybe Claire Cacciaguida could make some suggestions. She was a woman, and she wouldn't ask any embarrassing questions. Claire was OK!

He dialed the Network offices and got Claire. "Allo Claire, mon choux, could you please help me out of a small problem?"

Claire suspected that this was not going to be a business problem. Pepe was renowned for his peccadillos and she was relieved to hear that his problem only required her advice. She gave him the name and telephone number of a decorator whom she had consulted to furnish Carmine's apartment.

"By the way," Pepe added, as he thanked her, "I saw someone very interesting in the elevator of the Ansonia today, as I was leaving. I got on the elevator on the third floor, where my new apartment is, and who should be going down from a higher floor? Got any ideas?"

Claire chewed on her Juicy Fruit gum and replied, "Mother Teresa, arm in arm with Attila the Hun?"

"No but very close. It was Bidetto Passalacqua, one of the guys who disappeared after the last hit on the Dime Bank in Brooklyn. What would he be doing in the Ansonia?"

Claire had her suspicions since Iz Milocchio lived on the sixth floor of the Ansonia, but she did not share them with Pepe.

Pepe's thoughts returned to his new apartment. He would simply have the decorator buy the furnishings and he'd send her a check. This new apartment seemed better all the time. After Jasmine left, he could use it instead of hotel rooms for Heather, his latest girlfriend.

Having dealt with the apartment and its furnishings, Pepe reflected again on his poor Haitian wife who missed him and pleaded for a few moments of his time for herself and their children. He felt, for a moment, sad that he had devoted so little time to their care aside from the financial support that he gave them, which was more than ample for their needs in Haiti. He remembered Jasmine's gentle caresses, her warmth, and her admiration and need for him.

He did not know that as soon as she hung up the telephone after her tearful pleading, she relaxed and smiled. A few days earlier, she sat on the toilet in her apartment, looking intently at the pregnancy test stick. Her pretty face turned from anxious to angry. "Merde" was all she could bring herself to say, but she thought, "I'm two weeks late with my period now. I better get there tout suite and screw mon mari."

Chapter 22

Sam Testabuona walked briskly to the Bensonhurst Network office. Today was Monday and he'd be busy. Every weekday each MCO sent a list of its new claims to Claire at Network headquarters. She would break down these reports and send each Network branch a list of claims for its territory. Each new claim needed to be verified by the Network before it was paid. Sam Testabuona was one of the Bensonhurst gang's claims adjusters. Mondays were busy because they covered claims for crimes reported for the preceding weekend.

One case, Crimicaid number 1004729, was from a woman who submitted a claim for a mugging, with injuries to her face, legs and chest. The total claim was for seventy eight thousand dollars. He checked out her place. Through the garage window, he could see the rear end of a small red car. The front had a sheet over it.

Sam moved to the side of the garage, saw that the door had no deadbolt lock, and with a deft movement of a credit card had the door open in seconds. With the cover removed, he could see that the car was an Apgar Six, the new North Korean nuclear car Americans were importing to deal with their addiction to oil. Finally, U.S. policy had come up with a solution to that country's nuclear stockpile. It became more lucrative for them to sell nuclear cars than to extort the rest of the world with their nuclear capabilities.

Sam saw that the driver's side of the car was pushed in. The windshield was broken and there was blood on it, no doubt from where someone's head had hit it. The steering wheel was bent. Sam took photos of the damage, noted the location and time in his worksheet, and was gone in a few moments, careful to lock the door of the garage behind him. "Pretty good job," he thought, "Bullshit claim. Looks like she was mugged by her car, not a mugger. Seventy eight thousand dollars saved."

The other claims that day seemed legit, and by two PM, Sam had talked to the other victim-claimants, got what information he could on the perpetrators, and was ready to submit his Claim Investigation forms.

He sat in his swivel chair, just wide enough for his broad rump, and booted up his laptop. With his thick right index finger he slowly picked at the keys. On this woman's claim form, Sam checked the box in front of, "Recommend denial of claim." He paused before entering his findings in the box for an explanation. *"Does bullshit have one or two Ls?"*

Chapter 23
Katie Kewtie

Katie led Carmine into the studio with its fake window with a picture of the New York City landscape in the background. Two upholstered chairs awaited them and Katie ushered Carmine into one as she took the other. Her short dark hair framed the top of her smiling attractive face which was expertly made up to minimize the early cat whisker wrinkles at the corners of her mouth. The result was an appearance ten years younger than her forty two years. Katie had the optimistic and positive presence to put her guests at ease.

Carmine had been treated to his first make-over by Katie's makeup artist who applied a dab under each lower eyelid to lessen the dark shadows and give him a more youthful appearance. With his approval, she had also shortened his sideburns "just a tad." Carmine's serene exterior belied the anxiety that his sweaty palms and armpits would have given away if they had been visible to the thousands of people who would watch this interview.

Katie had cautioned him beforehand to look either at her, or at either of the two cameras but not at the lights that would make him squint.

The bright lights were turned on. Katie crossed her legs and switched from "Carmine" back to "Mr. Cacciaguida."

"Mr. Cacciaguida, thanks for joining us on AM Prime Time. Our viewers will, I'm sure, be as eager to meet you as I am. The news lately has been full of talk about Managed Crime and your leadership of it. Early reports are that it's working. But what problems still worry you?"

Suddenly, Carmine had to speak. He was surprised at his voice, resonant and assured. "Our network is a professional and disciplined organization. But we need to get a better handle on amateurs and individual criminals who aren't in the Network and still commit crimes. Also, we need to do a better job with domestic violence and crimes of passion. As more people enroll in managed crime plans we'll have more resources to spend on these issues. We'll increase our educational programs and counseling services."

Katie's brow wrinkled. "Education and counseling services have been around for a long time. What makes you think you can be successful where others have failed?"

Carmine could feel a trace of a grin appearing at the corners of his mouth, "Our counselors will be better motivators."

Katie's smile broadened, "You mean like "Big Louie the jawbreaker?"

Carmine became more serious. "Not exactly, big Louie's been replaced by smart young men dressed in suits and ties who are happy to explain to these amateurs why it's no longer in their interest to commit crimes. It's no longer only the police that they'll have to deal with and the Network is serious about keeping them from doing crimes."

Katie's eyes sparkled. "So it's Big Louie in a suit and tie? He's still going to break a jaw or two to convince them, right?"

"We can let them know that the Network will be very unhappy with jerks who continue to commit violent crimes, but we'll resist the urge to crack heads. We plan to help some of the amateurs find other jobs. A few of the bright and motivated ones might even be recruited for jobs with room for advancement in the Network. We'll need teams of investigators to find the perpetrators and counsel them. Who would be better at this than former crooks?"

Katie's skepticism was now apparent, "So you're going to make choirboys out of these crooks? What about all the ones who can't be converted? What are you going to do with them?"

Carmine had thought this problem through and was prepared. "Good question, Katie. Those that we can't convince to go straight, we'll report to the police, and we'll do all we can to see that they go to jail. We expect that there won't be many."

Katie was no pushover and wanted to ensure that no one could accuse her of coddling the subjects of her interviews, "Mr. Cacc, Carmine, managed crime pays criminals not to commit crimes. Do you see any parallels between managed crime and protection rackets?"

Carmine's palms were sweaty again. "We have a long history of paying farmers not to plant certain crops to control production when there is an oversupply. HMOs pay health care providers a fixed amount whether or not they provide services in order to prevent over-utilization. We're doing the same thing with crime."

Katie took a different tack, "Let's say you continue to succeed. Only some types of crime are covered by managed crime contracts. Do you think other types of crime such as drug trafficking, prostitution, and terrorism could someday be covered under managed crime plans?"

Carmine took a thoughtful pause, faced the nearer camera and replied, "As new crime management networks develop in other regions, we'll join forces and have the geographic coverage to deal with the vast and wealthy international drug cartels. Then we'll disrupt their hard drug distribution systems in this country."

"What about soft drugs and what about prostitution? You left them out."

Carmine replied softly, "I think we need to re-evaluate our attitude towards marijuana, gambling, and the sex trade. These businesses have prospered in spite of governmental repression because there's a demand for them. As long as there's a market, it'll be supplied by entrepreneurs. Maybe it's time to rethink our laws on soft drugs and prostitution."

Katie probed on. "Then what do **you** think we should do about dope and prostitution?"

Carmine replied in a firm voice, "We tried to control alcohol and failed with prohibition. Now, we allow and tax alcohol and tobacco, both far more dangerous than marijuana. As of two years ago, we had two million people in jails and prisons in this country. One in every one hundred and twelve men and one in every seventeen hundred and twenty women was sentenced to state or federal prisons in that year. It took five hundred thousand custody and security officers to care for them in the U.S. correctional system, and half again as many professional, technical, educational, clerical, maintenance, food service, and administrative workers to care for them. We are the most incarcerating country in the western world."

"So, you're suggesting that we legalize marijuana and prostitution?"

"If we want to reduce crime, the first thing we need to do is to be more selective about whom we lock up. We need to pick on what really is important and hurts people. We need to avoid the mistakes we made with prohibition and legalize marijuana, all forms of consensual sex between adults, and gambling. Marijuana is the most popular illegal drug in America. Marijuana is used more frequently than all other illegal drugs combined. More than two million people smoke it every day. If we locked them all up, we'd double the prison population."

"But isn't that just playing into the hands of drug cartels in Central America and the Far East? Won't we be swamped by tons of marijuana coming across our borders?"

Carmine was in his element and was beginning to enjoy this interview. "Much of the marijuana smoked here is grown right here in the U.S.A. and most of that is grown in the Midwest by clean-cut American farmers, not by Colombian cartels. The result of our war on marijuana has been to drive up the price so that it is a very profitable underground industry. Not only does this huge industry go un-taxed, but we pay taxes for the cost of catching, sentencing, and incarcerating the fifty thousand growers, sellers, and users currently in our jails and prisons."

Katie sounded surprised, and at the same time, worried "Well, what about prostitution, certainly not a victimless crime. These women are subjected to abuse and illness."

"Katie, as for the world's oldest profession, I think we would be better off legalizing it, taxing it, and using the proceeds to try to prevent sexually transmitted disease. The biggest problem with prostitution is the current worldwide epidemic of children and women being stolen or tricked into it and being kept as sex slaves. Legalizing it would give us entry into these businesses and help us to identify and save these captive women and children. The international groups that enslave women and children need to be put away and the freed women and children will need counseling and other support to reshape their lives. As for gambling, it's legal when governments run it. It's a great revenue stream for the Native Americans. I believe gambling should be open to other entrepreneurs as long as they're willing to pay their fair share of taxes on the proceeds."

While the cameras were fixed on Carmine, Katie decided that it was time to agree to disagree. She looked at the note card in her palm, and when Carmine had finished, she asked, "In your topsy-turvy world, where bad is good and good is bad, where crooks are good, and cops may be bad, do you believe there are good people and bad people?"

"Katie, tigers eat meat and cows eat grass. Is one good and the other bad? People can eat meat or vegetables. We have a choice. Within each of us is the capacity to do evil when the circumstances are right, like when we're convinced that we're in power, we're anonymous and will never be discovered, and that we'll never be punished, and especially when we've been taught that our victims are really less than human. We're also capable of selfless kindness to others even at risk to our lives and safety. Our culture right now revels in violence, on TV, in movies, in the news media, and in sports. Managed crime is designed to align people's success in life with avoiding violent behavior. We're an example that we won't tolerate violence, and that's definitely good!"

Katie smiled, "Carmine. There's something about you that makes me wonder what plans you have for the future. Could your plans include public service?"

Carmine looked directly at Katie, "I see myself in the service of the public right now. I think that working with the Network to control crime is the best thing I could be doing with my time."

Katie looked right back at him, "Any thoughts on an elected office?"

Carmine shook his head," I've enjoyed working with our state and federal legislators, especially United States Senator Payne Strong and New York City Mayor Fiorella LaGuardia and I appreciate all of their work in implementing the legislation necessary to reduce violent crime. I wish them all well; I would welcome the opportunity to continue working with them and I don't want any of their jobs."

Katie signaled the end of the interview. "Carmine Cacciaguida, it's been a treat having you with us today and I wish you the best of luck, for all of our sakes, in your efforts to control crime. Good luck. "

"Thanks Katie. It's been my pleasure."

With the TV segment recorded, the lights dimmed as Katie rose from her chair, shook Carmine's hand, smiled, and asked, "I notice you stopped at Senator. You never mentioned President. Why?"

Carmine left the question open "I'm already living in a dream or a pipe dream. When I find out which, I'll think more about the future."

Chapter 24

Pepe's little daughters ran to him, each threw her hands around one of his legs and waited for his kisses and hugs. He picked them both up, held one in each arm, and alternately kissed and bounced them to their great delight.

Jasmine, in high heels, got to him just a few seconds later. The girls looked bigger than he remembered: They were five and seven years old.

Jasmine was more beautiful than he remembered and seemed to have gained a little weight in some attractive places.

Pepe had remembered to put an assortment of new clothing in his closet and toilet articles in the bathroom. The refrigerator and pantry however, were bare. He would have to do some shopping quickly to give the place a more lived-in look.

He went out to a small grocery store while Jasmine and the girls unpacked.

Jasmine found her diaphragm in her purse and tossed it out of the bedroom window. She had never used one with Pepe. Why should she have one now?

She placed recent pictures of herself and the kids on the dressers in the apartment's two bedrooms and one on the door of the refrigerator. "Strange," she thought, "that the refrigerator was totally empty. It looked like he never ate in the apartment. Good. No need to change that. They would all eat out tonight."

A few hours later, she and her husband were side by side in bed, each admiring the youthful splendor of their spouse's body. Pepe marveled at her rounded breasts, wondering if they were even more attractive than he remembered, and if their nipples were a little more prominent?

The next morning, Jasmine arose early, before Pepe. She threw up briefly in the toilet, brushed her teeth, took her vitamins, had some toast and tea from the food that Pepe had bought yesterday, and took a taxi to Saks Fifth Avenue. She would have only a week or so to shop for a new wardrobe in New York City before she planned to return to Haiti.

Chapter 25

Every Thursday, there was a Continuing Education presentation for the Network's claims adjusters. Sam Testsabuona, like all of the others, needed fifty credit hours of continuing education every year to keep up his CMO claims adjuster license. The Network branches alternated in sponsoring meetings on subjects relevant to their current jobs.

Today, it was Jaime Poquito's branch and the topic was car theft. They met in a small auditorium at the YMCA in the Bronx. Six driver's side front doors of various model cars were lined up on low platforms. Several standard tools for jimmying the doors were there.

Sam entered the auditorium and greeted members of the other branches and snickered. He would bet that nobody in the room needed any instruction in using these tools.

Jaime began the program. He pointed out the chipped paint and the slightly out of shape edges of the doors that had been broken into with the various crude implements. His softly accented English and serious tone showed a respect for the process of entering the cars and also for ways of detecting that a car had been broken into.

Next, Jaime showed them the newest tool for getting into autos with keyboard entry systems. It was a T-shaped apparatus called a NAS-T about the size and shape of a garage door opener.

"You push the button here, it goes through a bunch of signals until it finds the correct combination, and the door lock opens. No signs of forced entry. These don't leave any evidence."

Next on the agenda was a short video on the workings of chop shops. It showed how quickly cars could be shed of their most valuable parts, and taken to the crusher.

In the pile of cars entering the crusher, Sam could clearly see the emblem Caprice Classic on the rear of a red Chevy as it was about to be crushed.

The location of the chop shop and the crusher were carefully not shown but Sam recognized the man running the crusher. It was Bidetto Passalacqua.

Chapter 26

At lunch with Harlan, Wayne stroked his moustache, a sign that he was about to ask an impertinent question, "So the chick that Carmine Cacciaguida lives with, did you check her out? She's real young and real good-looking. What's the scoop? Is she a gold digger or what?"

Harlan replied, "Her real name is Magdalena Limberger. She grew up in Wichita Falls, Texas. Her father was an oil driller and died when she was six years old. She was raised by her mother who was killed in a flood when Limber was sixteen years old."

"Pretty tough, losing both her parents so young. What'd she do? How'd she survive?"

Harlan continued, "Well, she moved into a high school friend Sarah's house. Limber was a top student in high school and then moved with Sarah, to Houston where they both studied modeling for a year.

Next, Limber moved to Austin, studied math at the University of Texas and graduated with honors. All the while, she supported herself with modeling jobs. After college, she joined a top Modeling Agency in New York City and does shoots for the Victoria's Secret catalog."

Wayne took another bite of his double classic burger, wiped catsup off his moustache "How did she and Carmine hook up?"

Harlan mused "That's still a mystery. It's not for his money. She lives at the Dakota and makes over three hundred fifty K's a year. Top credit rating. Doesn't smoke, drink, or use drugs. No criminal record. Seems to live within her means. Quiet. Not flashy when she's not working. May be ambitious. Maybe she likes the notoriety. Maybe she likes Carmine."

Chapter 27

Limber picked up the phone in her apartment and dialed.

"Hello. Is this Columbia University, Political Science Department? My name is Magdalena Limberger. I'd like to apply for admission to your graduate program next semester. Yes, I graduated from The University of Texas, Austin. I finished three years ago. I majored in mathematics. Magna cum laude. No, I don't think I'll need financial assistance. I'm not in school now. Self-employed. Model. I'll send you the application and my college transcript as soon as possible. Why would you need my portfolio? Maybe it would be best if a woman faculty member could do my interview!

Carmine tapped in the numbers on the phone in his apartment.

"Hans Bruder? Hans, this is Carmine Cacciaguida. How are you? And how's your sister, Greta? Schwester Bruder is also OK? Good. What are you two up to? A restaurant with beer and wurst? The worst wurst in Yorktown?"

"Listen, I hear you and Greta are interested in joining our network?

Well, "maybe" is a start. Your names came up at the last Network meeting. I asked Iz Milocchio and Nat Barth to contact you and find out just how interested you are in joining. Maybe they could tell you about the benefits of the Network and discuss how we operate. If it looks promising, we would bring it up it at the next meeting and possibly begin serious negotiations with you."

"Whatever you do, go look at our new prototype model pizzeria and legitimate money laundromat, Transafata Gigapizza. Iz has the first one of these. They're going to have special high-temperature super fast ovens to reduce baking time and lock in the flavor. All Network members will get free access to franchise rights. They'll be all over the city."

"Chuck, Chuck Baillie, this is Carmine Cacciaguida. Long time no see. How are things in Chicago? What? Your new toy store American Molls didn't go over big? Even with the outfits, the bullet-proof vests, the accessories, the stolen jewelry, the guns, the bullet-ridded cars, the toy banks and liquor stores to rob? No kidding! Kids today have no imagination!"

"I know it's hard to believe but things are going gangbusters. No, not literally. Listen, Chuck, this spring our New York Network is having a seminar. We're starting to make money and business is getting less risky every day. We've even got an offer from the local FBI to join up. Not only that, but we get to be the good guys with the white hats. No more paying off politicians. Could you ask for more? This is a real opportunity to look at new ways of operating. I'm asking the major players east of the Mississippi to come meet with us. We can fill you in on how we divide the revenue and how we manage to keep from killing each other. Are you at all interested in seeing how we work it? Good! We'll keep in touch about details."

"Miguel, this is Carmine Cacciaguida from New York. How are things in Houston? Too many foreigners? Can't be sure how Texas elections will go anymore? Want immigration reform? Miguel, you've got to learn how to get along.

The New York Network is having a................You're west of the Mississippi? I'm a New Yorker. What do we know about geography? How about east of the Rio Grande? Does that do it? We need Texas."

Andy Buonocore was in bed with his mistress Tina at her apartment. The phone rang and, Tina rolled over, picked it up and handed it to Andy, "Here, it's for you."

"Hello. This is Andy Buonocore. .....Why'd you call me here? You called me at home and my wife gave you this number? Marda! What's so important, you called me here? Giglio? What! I've been a lifter for ten years. You want me to be a capo this year? Am I honored? I'm fucking exploding with pride! I dreamed of this all my life. You bet I'll be there! Wild skunks cou'n't keep me away. The first planning meeting is next Tuesday? I'll be there. And please thank the guys for electing me."

Chapter 28

The Bruders' chosen meeting place was the Transafata Gigapizza on Christopher Street, corner of Bleecker Street, in the heart of Greenwich Village. It occupied the lower two floors of an apartment house, and its façade sported an illuminated sign with the letters T, F, and G, respectively in red, white, and green, the colors of the Italian flag. The ground floor featured a small seating area, cash registers, and the kitchen, which included three extra large pizza ovens, wider and taller than the usual ones. A stairway led to a larger space upstairs with Formica-topped tables and chairs. Iz, Nat, Hans, and Greta sat at a table, overlooking the enterprise.

Milocchio was pleasant and welcoming but somewhat uncomfortable, his fingers tapping the table top "Greta, Hans, let's go over the basics first. Nat, chime in if you have something to add."

Nat, a tall, athletic African American with a short afro, and the letters "MF" tattooed on the knuckles of his left third and fourth fingers, signaled Milocchio to go on.

Iz continued. "The Network is organized as a Limited Liability Company. It contracts with insurance companies that insure their customers against violent crime. The insurance companies pay the network sixteen dollars per month for each insured person."

Hans, a burley and affable Swiss with a large double chin, ran his hand over his close cropped brown hair, smiled, and with just a trace of an accent, said, "So far, so good."

As Nat looked at Hans, he imagined him as a St. Bernard with a small keg of beer under its chin.

Milocchio put both arms on the table, leaned toward Hans, and continued "If any covered person is the victim of a crime, the insurance company pays damages to the victim and subtracts the amount it pays from the Network's next paycheck."

"That's not zo good" grumbled Greta, in a much more pronounced accent than her brother's and both arms folded in front of her. Her high-pitched voice, staccato speech and diminutive body, reminded Nat of an angry, barking dachshund.

Milocchio kept his attention focused on Hans, who appeared more receptive than his sister. "The Network pays each of its member organizations according to how many people in its area are covered. The hardest part of the early stages was to negotiate these service areas. If you join, we'll have to work this out to include you."

Hans seemed interested and moved his chair closer to Milocchio. "Interesting. With whom do Greta and I negotiate what our service area will be?"

Nat also leaned toward Hans trying to be reassuring, but sounding as if he were speaking to children. "Hans, Iz and I will give you a real good deal. You and Greta won't have nothin' to worry your little heads about."

Greta, raised her five foot one inch frame out of her chair, stared at Nat, and barked, "Watch out with der little heads, Mr. Pumpernickel. Hans and I will worry about exactly what **we** want to worry about. So what's with this shtupid Lotsa Fata Pizzeria?"

Milocchio was even more soothing. "Let's all stay calm; we'll have plenty of time to argue later. Please cool it, Nat. Maybe Hans and I should do the negotiating. Greta, let me explain. The pizza business is a franchise. It's free to Network members.

The Network has the brand and acts as a buying consortium to get really good prices on the ingredients. So each of these places makes money in a largely cash business. There are tax advantages. Also, the pizzerias can serve as a means of washing money from other sources that are still not so legal, not that you would be involved in any such ventures."

Hans grinned, "So the pizzeria is a washeteria?"

Nat ignored Hans' joke, "Sorry to have rattled your Aryan teapots," and continued in mock humility, "I apologize for being condescending. I won't do that again." and then seriously, "But all this talk of pizza has got me hungry. Iz, how about we see just how fast this pizza is gonna' get here?"

Within moments pizza arrived. Hans tasted a slice, and smiled, "Not bad! Pepperoni is nice, but in Yorkville, we'd have to try a pizza with schnitzel. What do you think, Greta?"

Greta ate a slice, wiped her mouth with a napkin, yawned, and covered her mouth with her hand. "I think that all this talking is making me tired. We better get home."

Hans caught the yawn from Greta, "You're right schwester, I'm also tired. Funny, it's not even ten o'clock yet."

A little while later, Milocchio shoveled the contents of an oven into a trash bag. "Ashes to ashes, dust to dust. These ovens are fast!"

Nat was enjoying the moment immensely. "Hansel an' Gretel didn't make it out of **this** gingerbread pizza joint without going through the oven. Whoa! The mutha' had an artificial hip. Look at that thing sitting in the pile of ashes with the melted silver fillings from their teeth!"

Milocchio: "Titanium. It has a very high melting point, much hotter than this oven. Carmine would be angry if he knew the details of this meeting."

"Tough!" said Nat, "Just say they weren't interested. OK?"

Chapter 29

Giglio means "lily" in Italian, but in Brooklyn, the Giglio also refers to a sixty five foot high brightly painted, gracefully tapered tower, which is the main attraction in the festival of that name. This week-long celebration, the Giglio, happens the third week of every July. The Giglio which weighs two tons, is repeatedly picked up by a group of one hundred twenty lifters, carried short distances, and put down again. This Dance of the Giglio celebrates Saint Paulinus, the patron saint of Nola, Italy, The tower is built on a framework of aluminum, covered with panels of papier mache decorated with saints, lilies, angels, birds, and a Madonna. On top is a statue of Saint Paulinus.

Only the strongest men in the neighborhood get to be lifters. Andy Buonocore had been a lifter for ten years. But the Giglio was organized and run by three leaders called capos. His whole life, Andy wanted to be a capo. His uncle Giuseppi had been a grand capo, which was number one and the highest honor one could get in the neighborhood. To be a capo, a man had to be respected, and it helped to have enough money to be generous to the parish. Andy was thrilled to have been elected to be a capo.

Andy knew from watching all those years, that he would take his capo cane, step out in front of the Giglio, and signal the band to begin. The music would start. On the last note, he would lift his cane straight up in the air and the lifters would go from a crouching position under the Giglio to standing up straight. They would jerk the Giglio off its supports, up into the air. The crowd would roar. He would jerk the cane upwards again, and the Giglio would move forward. He would walk backward, watching that the Giglio did not tip, and gesture with the cane, giving instructions to keep it straight. When they got to the end of the lift, he would shout commands, the lifters would bend their knees, ducking all at once, and the Giglio would come down hard onto its supports. The crowd would cheer wildly.

That was what should have happened. But soon after he got the call, and five months before the festival was scheduled to begin, Andy went to a pre-Giglio planning meeting and began having weakness in his legs. An hour later, he couldn't stand up. The head capo called an ambulance which took him to Maimonides Medical Center. By the time he got there, he had trouble moving his fingers.

He underwent an MRI, blood tests, and a spinal tap. When the results of the tests were back, the neurologist told Andy that he had ascending paralysis, called Guillain Barre syndrome. The prognosis was good for eventual recovery, but the disease was still getting worse and nobody could predict how severe his paralysis would be or whether it would involve his breathing muscles. If he wasn't able to breathe on his own, he would require a tube in the throat and a ventilator. In a few hours he had gone from planning his greatest feat, to being paralyzed. By the next morning, Andy had lost the use of his arms and couldn't feed himself. He was embarrassed that someone would have to wipe his ass.

But most of all, he worried about who would watch over his not so legal, non-Managed Crime business interests and those of his employees in his Brooklyn enterprise. Who would run his mob when he was recovering or worse, if he never recovered?

Chapter 30

On the evening of the next day, Limber was relaxing on the divan in her living room. Her feet were on the coffee table and the New York Times News of the Week in Review was on her lap. A soft tap on her apartment door surprised her. Most visitors rang the bell and had to identify themselves on the intercom before she buzzed them into the building. Carmine had a key but he always called before coming over.

Perplexed, she went to the door and was surprised to see Carmine through the peephole.

She opened the door quickly and gave him a hug. "Come on in Carmine. You look real upset! What's wrong? How's Andy?"

Carmine's attempt to control his emotions was belied by a wavering in his voice. Limber hadn't seen him so distressed. She put her arms around him.

"Not much is right today Limber. Andy is almost totally paralyzed. He can't use his hands, arms, or legs; he can only say a few halting words. At least he can breathe on his own and his son, Dante says he has a good chance to recover."

Limber responded to Carmine's distress by hugging him tighter and gently stroking his scalp. Carmine took hold of her hand in his and added, "But I can tell Andy's real worried about how to control the Brooklyn business. He doesn't project much of a powerful image right now to handle the types who collect on bad debts and make sure we, I mean they, get paid. He needs someone to take over for him for a while, until he gets better." Carmine let go of her hand and sank into the couch.

Limber didn't like the direction in which Carmine seemed to be going. "What about Lou Cannone, his right hand man? or his son Dante?"

Carmine's voice was anguished. "Lou's too ambitious and not smart enough. Andy doesn't trust him. Dante is busy being a doctor and doing research on stem cells in the brain. There's no one. He wants me to help for a while."

Limber jerked erect, and her face turned from concerned to angry as she glared at Carmine. "Over one of our dead bodies, and I'm not sure it would be mine! If you think I came here to New York to live with some rich hoodlum, you've got the wrong heifer. I came here to be with the most interesting man in the United States of America, a man who was doing more good than anyone I know or have heard of. That's supposed to be you, Joseph Carmine!"

Carmine, trying to regain his composure, began to explain, "Andy is my oldest and best friend."

Limber cooled down a bit and tried a more reasoned approach. "Look how hard you worked to get out of all of that! Do you really want to be involved in cracking heads and shooting kneecaps? Is that what you want? Do you want blood on your hands? If you're going to have dirty hands, keep them out of my apartment."

Carmine remembered being scolded by his mother long ago for having expressed "irreverent" thoughts about a girl in his seventh grade class, and felt the same sense of shame now. Limber was right. But before he could admit it, Limber continued, "I don't want to be bailing you out. I want, some day, to be working on your campaign for the presidency of this country. You can't run for president from jail."

Carmine was contrite, and smiling now, "Magdalena Limberger, Magda, you amaze me. You sure **you** don't want to run Andy's business?"

Magda stood above Carmine, who was still seated on the divan, and stroked the back of his neck. "No chance! If you don't run for president, maybe I will. I may not have the name recognition you have," and, impishly, "but my face is recognizable and my boobs are right up there."

Carmine pulled her down to him so that their lips almost met. "Looks like this Limber won't bend. You'll always be Magda to me now."

Magda smiled, "Since we're now talking about always, candidates for president usually do better with a wife and kids than with a girlfriend. I don't want to rush you, but we have to think ahead."

Chapter 31

In his FBI office, Harlan Dreyfus had just buffed his shoes and was replacing the polish and brush in his desk drawer when the phone rang.

"Dreyfus?" said the female voice at the other end, "This is Claire Cacciaguida."

He quickly tried to remove a spot of errant shoe polish from his hand as he juggled the phone. He frowned. "What happened to Harlan? Suddenly I'm Dreyfus again?"

"That's right," she replied, "I'm going to be really busy for the next while and it needs to be strictly business between us. Do you understand?"

"No, but you sound serious so I won't argue the point."

"Right again." she said, "So if you still want to talk to Carmine, you'll have to arrange it yourself."

"OK and I do still want to see Carmine. And I will still call you if I hear anything that makes me think that Carmine's in danger."

Claire's voice was a little less hurried but still serious. "Much appreciated, but that's going to be the only type of contact we can have. Carmine knows you want to see him. You can give him a call yourself."

"Remember, if you get less busy any time soon, please give me a call," he said with concern.

Claire's voice softened, "Would you bail me out? Bye now."

Claire dialed Carmine's number. "Dad, tell Andy I'll do it. I'll cover for him."

Carmine felt a hint of wetness in his eyes, "Claire, that's the first time you called me Dad in years. Thanks, sweetheart. I love you. Be careful." He wished for a moment that Bernice was still alive so she might feel less bothered that she hadn't given him a son. Claire was everything he could wish for.

"Just a slip." Claire quipped, "Don't go all mushy on me now, just when we have to hang tough. I'll go over to see Andy. I hear he won't need to be on a ventilator. Dante thinks they will let him out of the hospital in a few weeks. Is that right?"

Carmine was glad to be on the phone rather than talking in person to his daughter. He could wipe away the tears without hiding them from her. "Seems to me he looks a little better."

Chapter 32

Basel, Switzerland can be cold in March, especially at night. A bitter cold wind blew against the façade of the Euler Hotel, on Centralbahnplatz, in the heart of the old town. Each of the hotel's sixty-four rooms was adorned with antiques and fine art. It was the ritziest hotel in Basel.

Across Centralbahnplatz, in a small hotel facing the Euler, a sharpshooter's telescope was barely visible between the edges of the window curtain. Hans Schlepf, the occupant of the room on which the scope was fixed, did not see the scope. He was too busy trying to maintain an erection of his sixty-five year-old penis. His eighteen year-old female companion had fled with him from France when the French government confiscated his food additive factory and other property for back taxes. He had also neglected to fund the pension plan of his employees. Nor did he pay his servants, shopkeepers, and his main brothel. So, Schlepf had many enemies.

The man with his eye to the scope was Facciabrutta, a Maltese assassin. Facciabrutta didn't know or care which of Schlepf's enemies had hired him. His usual fee, one million Euros, had been deposited in his numbered Swiss bank account.

With his scope fixed on Schlepf, Facciabrutta fondled the switch on the transmitter. He had adjusted it to the frequency needed to activate the solenoid on the wiring of the electric blanket now pushed down on the bed, with only Schlepf's right big toe touching it, one of his hands gripping the metal bedpost. Facciabrutta waited for the moment when the girl got out of bed and went into the bathroom. Then, he closed the switch which activated the solenoid on the blanket. Schlepf uttered a muffled grunt as the high amperage of the 240 volts electric current created havoc with the conduction system of his heart and stopped its orderly beating. In a few seconds, Schlepf was dead. Facciabrutta opened the switch, the wiring reverted to normal, and the girl noticed nothing when she got back into bed with her seemingly sleeping elderly lover. When she awoke the next morning, all would believe that he had died of natural causes, probably a coronary event.

Facciabrutta packed up his scope and a small suitcase and, one hour later, sat comfortably on his flight out of Basel. No one would connect him with the repairman who had come to Schlepf's room to repair a light switch three days earlier. In fact, nobody would even remember his being there. Facciabrutta's appearance, in spite of his name, ("ugly face" in Italian,) was so average, so without distinguishing features, that scarcely anyone noticed him. People almost never remembered him.

No one remembered the wurst stand during last June's Fasnacht festival in Basel, where Hans Schlepf's brother Fritz bought his last bratwurst, or the very ordinary man at the stand who sold Fritz the bratwurst that, several hours later, caused Fritz' severe diarrhea and shock. The source of the enterotoxin-producing E. coli bacteria was never found and the local public health authorities were puzzled about this single fatal case of a disease that usually occurred in outbreaks involving at least several people who ate food from the same source.

At his home somewhere in Malta, was the ordinary-looking Facciabruta. The fake mole that he had worn on his nose in his early days as an assassin, along with the makings of the fake scar for his face, were safely hidden away.

Two hours later, in Malta, Facciabruta's cell phone rang.

"Please leave a message." said the computerized greeting on his phone.

The message was brief: "Your target is Carmine Cacciaguida, at the Freedom Tower on Good Friday. Assets transferred to your account."

Chapter 33

Carmine's and Claire's office was adjacent to the large wood paneled room where the Network held its meetings. He stood at his window overlooking the west side of lower Manhattan and the Hudson River. He could see the New Jersey shore and admire the distant tugboats ferrying larger ships back and forth.

In his hand was the one hundred fifty dollar parking ticket that greeted him as he returned to the double-parked Volt after a brief stop at Zegna's to pick up a suit. .

Carmine wondered whom to call to take care of the ticket. Mentally, he ticked through his list of political contacts. But, asking any of them for a favor for something as trivial as a parking ticket wouldn't be good for his image. So he wrote out a check, stuffed it in the envelope with the ticket, and put it in his pocket to mail later.

Carmine sat and speed dialed a number.

The phone rang in a large condo in Miami.

Carmine turned on the phone's speaker so any FBI bug could hear both sides of the conversation.

"Hello, Mrs. Bernstein", (pause) "Just tell him it's Carmine calling."

Any FBI agent listening to the call would have to imagine Abe Bernstein, saunter to the phone in his tennis shoes and T shirt with "NUMBER ONE GRAND PUTZ" printed on the rear. "Hey paysan! This is Abe. Cosa fa?"

"Abe Bernstein! Schmuck! Whad d'ya read?"

Abe scratched the shiny top of his head where seven hairs stretched from one side to the other, trying to do the work of thousands to cover his bald scalp. "Busy here in retirement in Miami. My wife's Hadassah group is having a dinner honoring Monica Lewinsky for her service to Jewish womanhood."

Carmine was puzzled, "Monica Lewinsky? Hadassah?"

Abe smirked, "One courageous oral act dispelled forever the infamous myth that Jewish women are sexually inhibited and will not perform certain unnatural sex acts."

Even in his later years Abe was amusing and still a fox. "So, if they're reconciled to Monica Lewinsky, how do they feel about Bill Clinton? How do they feel about a guy who would take advantage of a young intern?

"My kid sister, Marilyn, has a picture of her and her husband on either side of Bill Clinton with his arms around her and her husband. It was taken right before he left office. Clinton was flying around the country thanking people who supported him early in his campaign. She had sent him a check for ten dollars and that got them into a picture with Clinton nine years later. I asked my sister if she was worried that being so close he might make a pass at her.

"She said 'Me, worried? He should have been worried about me. I would love to have grabbed him!' As for myself, I say 'What good is being president if you can't mess with an intern now and then?'"

"So Abe, tell me the truth. Can you get really good bagels down there in Miami? Does your mouth water once in a while for a nice Zabar's bagel, maybe with some belly lox and cream cheese? How about a pastrami sandwich on rye from the Stage Deli? I promise you both if you'll come here for a seminar on what we're doing here in New York with managed crime. You know about our network and Iwant to extend it. Players from all over the country are coming. It will be in April. How about it?"

"Well, as you know," Abe replied, "I'm retired now, so I'm not exactly a player, but it might be interesting to hear what's going on. Keep in touch. And by the way, if I decide to come, make sure you got bialys, and a little cream cheese."

Carmine thought, *"Retired, my ass!"*

Carmine finished his sandwich and placed another call.

"Phillip, this is Carmine Cacciaguida in New York. We haven't met but I thought I'd call to invite you to a seminar we're having here. We're doing fine with our managed crime network and we're thinking of broadening our membership. Chuck Baillie from Chicago, Miguel from Houston, and Bernstein from Miami are coming and I'd sure like to have you join us from Atlanta so we can explain how things work, what our prospects are for the future, and how you might fit in."

Phillip Blake was a short, thin man whose family had lived in Atlanta since before the civil war. He was known to carry a small taser disguised as a fountain pen. The word was that he also had other concealed high tech weapons that only he knew about. "I heard about what y'all are doing in New York and I think you're nuts! Now that you've got another Mayor LaGuardia in New York City, I thought you would have your hands full making a living but y'all came up with a hare brained scheme. You expect me to believe that they actually pay you for doing nothing?"

This was not quite the response Carmine had expected but he had heard that Blake would not be easy to convince. "Phil, that's just the point! Fiorella is one of our biggest supporters. So is Senator Strong. Even the FBI is on our side. They want a seat on our Network board."

Blake was having none of it. "Aside from Strong, who's OK, if the rest of those guys are on your side, then you're on the wrong side. Call me when you wake up from your dream."

Carmine was careful. "I guess that means you're not coming, Phil?"

"I didn't say I'm not coming. I wouldn't miss this for anything. But call me once in a while to let me know you're still alive. Sho' nuf, somebody's bound to want to render you inactive, if you get my drift."

"I expect to be very much alive and will be happy to see you in April, at our meeting. It's been interesting talking with you."

Chapter 34

Wind-blown sheets of rain pounded the windows of the Network office.

Claire and Carmine were going over the burgeoning paperwork of dealing with the city, state, and federal governments.

"The Feds keep coming up with new crimes that we're expected to cover, "groaned Claire." Each of these has a Crime Procedure Table CPT number just like diseases have in health care. Then there are metrics for Crimicare to show that we're preventing crime. Now they want us to see if the counseling we are providing convicted felons before they leave prison is working. They want to know the percent that are reconvicted within two years of release from prison. Jaime and Nat visited yesterday and Jaime suggested that 'we give them **out of this world** counseling, if you get my drift.' Then, in his best mock preacher imitation, Nat pointed skyward and exhorted, 'Whoa man, hold off the whacking. What are we, a bunch of hoodlums?'"

Claire, continued, "Then there's the Managed Crime Financing Administration that's leaning on the CMOs for a breakdown of numbers of each crime by its CPT code every quarter.

"I'll bet that's driving up the admin costs," sympathized Carmine.

"It's also driving us crazy!" moaned Claire, "We're going to drive up the local cost of headache pills at the rate we're using them."

Carmine's voice was soft and questioning. "Iz called me today." He and Nat couldn't convince the Bruders to go along with us. The Bruders have disappeared and Iz and Nat are dividing their turf and hiring their people. I'm not happy with this outcome. Can't help wondering what happened to the Bruders. Iz says he doesn't know but I don't believe him.

Claire, still preoccupied by the added paperwork the cost of the added paperwork, mused, "I think we'll charge the CMOs another forty six cents per member per month for it."

"By the way Claire, is there any news from our personal FBI agent?" asked Carmine.

Claire shrugged, "He still wants to meet with you."

"If I can work with the devil, I suppose I can work with the FBI. Have him call me."

Chapter 35

Harlan's office had not changed much since he moved in. His Brown University and Stanford Law School diplomas now adorned the wall behind his desk. Wayne fidgeted in the chair facing him.

"Wayne, what's up? What's the rush?"

Wayne fingered his moustache. "Harlan, I need someone to vent to about my twelve year old daughter. She's couldn't wait to get boobs, and now that she's got 'em, she's pissed because they're too big for a ballerina. Her dance teacher wants her to go into modern dance where boobs are OK. She's been talking about being a ballerina for the last six years and now, she's talking about getting surgery to make them smaller.

"You came over here, to tell me about your daughter's boobs?!"

"Nah, I really gotta' tell you about this phone call that our terrorist surveillance group picked up last week from a cell phone with a GPS fix in Malta. The transcript read 'Carmine Cacciaguida is your target. Freedom Tower. Good Friday. Assets transferred to your account.' We have the number but can't connect the number to a person. It took them a week to figure out that this might be of more than routine interest. It sounds to me like an order for a hit on your favorite crook."

"Shit! It took them a week to figure that out? Are they still linked with that phone?"

"Yeh, but the phone's been quiet all week."

Harlan reached out and shook Wayne's hand. "I guess I'd better meet with Carmine."

Chapter 36

The brick clad four story house was one block off the boardwalk in Brighton Beach.

Claire took the elevator to the top floor, knocked, and was greeted by Mila Gryntzpan's outstretched chubby arms.

"Come in. Would you like a cup of chicken soup?" and without waiting, "I didn't think so. How about a cup of coffee?" She took Claire's coat and hung it over a chair.

Claire nodded an "OK" to the coffee and Mila ushered her to a plastic covered upholstered chair in the living room. Mila was apologetic about the plastic, mumbling about how messy the kids were. She left and returned with a paper cup of coffee. "These are the good paper cups, for company. My Yuri, God bless him, prays all day but doesn't want any strangers in the house to clean. Listen, Claire, thanks for coming all the way to Brooklyn to chat with an old woman. I've known your papa a long time. I respect what he's doing and I know what you're about to begin doing to protect Andy and him."

Between sips of strong coffee, Claire responded, "Thanks, Mila. Dad has always spoken highly of you but what exactly do you think I'm going to do and how does that concern you?"

Mila smiled and crossed her heavy thighs, "Pardon my being a busybody; I can't help it. Look, I know you're a smart girl, but I need to warn you about what you're getting into. My Brighton

Beach and Andy's Bensonhurst are right next to each other. I know a lot about the goings on there, and maybe a thing or two that even Andy doesn't know."

"I'm all ears, bubbie." said Claire, "You don't mind if I use a Yiddish word, do you?"

Mila laughed and her second and third chins vibrated. "Go right ahead. It's music to my ears, especially coming from your mouth. Listen, Louis Cannone, Andy's next in line, is a schmuck! He'll give you a lot of trouble if you're not careful. I wouldn't be surprised if he was stealing from Andy. I think he's not on the up and up about what he's getting into. He's violent and he's not a fan of the Network. There's also something fishy about the cops in his precinct, especially the lieutenant, Will Knap. I wouldn't put it past Cannone to do anything for more power. Watch out for him. I hope Andy gets back into action fast. And, if you need some help, don't stand on ceremony, call me."

Claire got up, the two women hugged, and Claire left.

A few moments later, Mila's phone rang. Mila had expected the call. One of her sex workers, passport in hand, had left Mila's brothel and set up her own enterprise only three blocks away. Freedom for her workers was a good thing, but not when it became competition.

"A small fire in her new place would be fine, to teach her a lesson," said Mila into the phone, but see nobody gets hurt."

Chapter 37

The Spumoni Gardens restaurant, between West Eleventh and Twelfth Streets in Bensonhurst, has been a landmark known for its square thick crust pizzas and spumoni and gelati for more than seventy-five years. Not at all elegant, it sat across the street from the low rent Marlborough housing project. The interior was casual, the service offhand, and the food was good. Claire sat at a Formica–topped table that wobbled as she leaned on it and poked at the salad on her plate. Across the table sat Lou Cannone, wearing a blue blazer and his one tie.

Lou wasn't happy. Claire was probing to find out how business was going. "Lou, how's your drug business doing?"

Lou uncrossed his arms, pulled out a Camel, lit it, and blew smoke in her face. "Marijuana, hash, and THC. That's all, if you're asking. We don't do no business within two blocks of any of the schools around here. We don't sell **nothing** to kids. Business from drugs is flat from last year."

Claire enjoyed the smoke and wished she could have a cigarette. "How about the gross take from numbers? Has the increase in government-run lotteries hurt our business?"

Lou was more irritated now, but wondered if there was a chance he could make it with her. "What's with the **our** business? I thought you were only watching 'til Andy gets back? We do OK.

So long as the cock-sucking state and the fucking feds tax the shit out of lottery winnings, we'll do good."

"I'm strictly temporary, Lou. I hope more than you do that Uncle Andy comes back real soon."

Nothing Claire said could calm Lou down. "He's not your fucking uncle, Claire," Lou shouted, "He's my fucking real uncle, my mother's brother. All he is to you is Carmine's friend. He can take his fucking time coming back as far as I care."

As revolting as Lou was to Claire, she nevertheless momentarily wondered what he would be like in bed.

Lou continued his tirade. "I do most of the work around here anyways. And your father, what a pussy with his managed crime shit! If the two of youse knew what you were doin', youse would be kicking my ass to get into all the things you're trying to keep me out of. Some fucking boss you'd make!"

Claire's brow wrinkled and her chin jutted out. "I've called him Uncle Andy for as long as I can remember, and he seems to like it. That's good enough for me."

Lou knew it was time to cool down. He dropped the cigarette on the floor and ground it out. "Look, Claire, this is getting boring. You got anything more you want to aks me about?"

Careful not to rock the table, Claire removed her hand from it, "One last thing, what's your take on the two robberies at the Dime Bank? Who do you think pulled them off and why haven't the cops done a real investigation on them? Do you know anything about them?"

"*No way to calm this down.*" Lou thought. He brought his fist down hard on the wobbly table. "What the fuck is this, the inquisition? I've been doing most of the fuckin' work around here for my uncle Andy and when shit happens, does he turn things over to me? No, he gives it to Carmine's daughter, who doesn't know shit! I'm sick of sitting around getting pussy-whipped by a stuck-up bitch with a PhD."

Claire had pushed him past the limit "Lou, it's been an experience, meeting you. What you lack in finesse, you make up for with charm."

Lou summarized the encounter with a single word, "Cunt!"

Durgayoni drove Clair back to Manhattan while Claire wished she could have one cigarette. "Dee, I just can't believe anything he says. Mila thinks he may be pushing hard drugs, and selling them to kids. He freaked out when I asked him about the bank heists, and he came down hard on Carmine and Andy. I think he knows a lot more than he's telling and, frankly, I think he may be dangerous to Andy and maybe even Carmine. Dreyfus seems concerned about Carmine's safety. He must have a reason."

Durgayoni hesitated, "Claire, you want answers, you need Devanta. He's an old friend, a Sikh. I can call him in Chandigarh, if you like."

Chapter 38

Devanta Singh was tall, slender, and had the distinction, in his childhood, of having the world's last known case of smallpox which left his dark-skinned face peppered with scars.

Devanta's flight from Chandigarh to Delhi and on to London gave him time to reflect on his telephone conversation with Durgayoni. It was eight years since they fell in love at the Punjab University in Chandigarh. Durgayoni spent four years at the Barli Development Institute for Rural Women in Indore, and had come to the University as a reader in the Faculty of Education. Devanta was already a professor in the Faculty of Pharmaceutical Sciences and Durgayoni was the prettiest, brightest and most strong-willed woman he knew. On the day four years ago that he planned to propose marriage to her, she announced she was leaving for New York. The engagement gift that he had for her was a gold broach with a star ruby that had belonged to his mother. He also took it with him when he visited her in New York City two years ago. Her ardor for him then had not lessened but she would not come back to India with him. The broach was again in his pocket. He was sure that this time, he would stay in New York and marry her if she would have him.

He had, several months ago, received an invitation to be a visiting professor at the New York University Medical School. They were interested in his work on genetic technology for the development of new antibiotics for drug-resistant bacteria and he suspected that with the invitation came a chance that he might be offered a faculty position there. His work was going well and he had delayed accepting the offer to visit. Now he had a reason to go to New York and they would pay his expenses.

He bought Durgayoni a box of Godiva chocolates in London's Heathrow Airport on the layover before his flight to New York. Did she still have a passion for chocolate?

On the flight, he wondered if the food in New York City would make him ill. He had taken along some Ciprofloxacin, just in case.

"Durgayoni said she needed me. Needed my special skills. Needed them right away. It was very important. What in my background could that be? I was twenty-one in nineteen eighty four when Indira Gandhi ordered the desecration of the Golden Temple in Amritsar, our holiest site. I worked for Sikh independence in the Akali Dal party for a few years while I was in pharmacy school and was trained in martial arts and weaponry for the movement. But I've been a researcher and a professor of pharmacology for years. Could it be my early work on drugs that affect the central nervous system that interests her?"

Chapter 39

Claire's townhouse had elegant white stucco walls, with black doors and shutters. Like all of the other houses on the block, it had an iron fence with a simple gate. Claire liked the sense of security that a fence gave.

Claire buzzed Durgayoni and Devanta through the gate and the front door.

Durgayoni smiled and introduced her Sikh friend, "Claire, this is my old beau, Devanta. He loves chocolate. He bought this box supposedly for me but he'll eat most of it."

Claire was struck by the scars on the man's otherwise handsome face as she ushered them into chairs. To Claire, they looked good together. "Devanta, Dee says you have ways of interrogating people to get information from them that they don't wish to divulge. Is that true?"

Devanta was not sure whether this pretty American woman was just a friend or a competitor for Durgayoni's affection. "True," he answered. "This was a routine chore in my days with the Sikh Independence Movement. There were cases where people's lives were at stake and we had to be able to tell friends from foes. We had pretty good luck in getting the truth."

Claire poured tea for her guests. "We have a problem. We need to know the truth from someone who works for our organization but who may also be betraying us. But he is a close relative of someone about whom we care and we wouldn't want him harmed. Do you have any ideas how we could get the information we need without hurting him?"

Devanta sipped the tea, nodded in approval, and said, "I can find out what you want, and when we're done, he won't even know what he's told you. Would that be adequate?"

Durgayoni beamed at Devanta, "A man after my own heart."

Devanta looked at her, "Precisely."

Chapter 40

Momma Cohen's Knish Factory was now familiar to Claire. On the top floor, above the knishes, the brothel, and the numbers, there was Mila's, office. And there sat Mila, looking very much like "Mama Cohen" along with Claire, Durgayoni, and Devanta Singh. Their attention was focused on a large leather sofa, on which lay an unconscious Lou Cannone. The date-rape drug had done its work and it was now up to Devanta. The others were engrossed as he removed Lou's trousers and boxer shorts, separated his buttocks, and cleansed the area of his anus with an alcohol swab. Devanta donned latex gloves, produced a container of intravenous five percent glucose in sterile water, attached it to tubing and a needle, and inserted the needle into a protruding large anal vein. He waited for Lou to stir. Just as Lou was beginning to awaken, Devanta injected drug into the hemorrhoid through the IV tubing.

Devanta explained, "Most middle aged people have a hemorrhoid or two. Very convenient for injecting the most modern combination of drugs that will get us the information we need without him remembering anything about this encounter and without leaving any telltale signs of our adventure on his skin."

Durgayoni was impressed and wondered, "What's in the IV, if it's not too secret to tell us?"

Devanta taped the needle in place in the hemorrhoid. "Some scopolamine so he won't remember, sodium pentothal to maintain just the right amount of sedation, and Verilox, a substance of my own design, that lessens inhibitions. Some people say peculiar things under the influence of these drugs, just like some do while under general anesthesia. That's one way of knowing that the drugs are working."

Mila had never been so intimately involved with any anus other than her own. She closed her gaping jaw and asked, "Boychik, why not just give him some schnapps? That's what schnapps does for my husband. I sure hope this stuff works; I really wanna know what this schmuck is up to."

Cannone moved his mouth, and softly repeated, "Schmuck. Schmuuck. Schmuuuck."

Devanta moved closer to Lou and spoke into his ear, "Lou, I'm going to ask you some questions. I know it may be hard to remember, but please try hard to think."

Cannone said softly, "Pussy. Puussy. Puuussy."

Claire was not impressed by the view of his anus and the scrotum in front of it. "He doesn't improve even when he's almost unconscious."

Devanta injected another minute amount of drug through the intravenous tubing. "Lou, what kinds of drugs do you sell?

Cannone responded so softly that the onlookers had to strain to hear him. "Everything. Coke, hash, heroin, acid, crystal, smack, crack, schmuck, and pussy. Everything."

Devanta patted Lou's arm, "Good boy. Where do you sell them?"

Cannone replied, a little louder, "Everywhere. Street, houses, candy stores, Brooklyn College, high schools, and across the street from the police station."

Devanta crooned, "Across from the police station? Isn't that dangerous?

Cannone spoke a little louder, "No, the lieutenant doesn't give a shit. Will Knap couldn't care less!"

Devanta asked, "Will Knap, is he the lieutenant?"

Cannone's voice was louder with each utterance, "He's the lieutenant. Schmuuuuck. Puuuussy. Margaret, the ice cream is melting. Put it in the fridge, Bitch."

Claire smiled at Durgayoni and Devanta, "Poor Margaret, whoever she is."

Mila smirked. "He's still a putz."

Cannone. "Putz. Puutz. Puuutz."

Devanta returned to business, "Why doesn't Knap care about your selling drugs?"

Cannone turned his head away from Devanta, who gave him more drug. Cannone replied, "He don't give a shit. He didn't even do any work on the two bank jobs. He hates the Network as much as I do. He says, "If crooks control crime, then who needs cops?" Also, he takes money."

Devanta, in a soothing tone, asked, "How do you know that?"

Cannone laughed softly, "Cause I give it to him, a thousand a month. He said someone else from the Network also gives him money but I don't know who it is. Could be Milocchio."

Devanta injected another small dose of drug, "Why do you give him money?"

Cannone briefly fell asleep, and finally responded, "Good for business."

Devanta thought he'd better hold off giving Cannone more drug for a while. "Does Andy know about the money?"

Cannone's voice was weak again, "No. He don't know shit."

Devanta enjoyed seeing the drug working, especially since Durgayni was watching. "You don't like the Network. What do you think of Carmine?"

Cannone responded, "Carmine's done for, won't be around much longer."

Devanta prodded on, "How do you know that?"

Cannone moved his head from side to side. "From Will Knap. That's what he thinks."

Devanta pushed more drug into the IV. "How does he know?"

Cannone replied, "I dunno."

Devanta turned to the others and asked, "Claire, do you have any other questions for him?"

Claire wanted very much for Devanta to ask one more question, "Sounds like there may be a hit on Carmine. Does he know anything about who ordered the hit?"

Devanta patted Lou's arm again to get his attention, "Lou, Do you know who ordered Carmine to be killed?"

Cannone mumbled, "No, but I think it's the same guy who paid off Will Knap and I think he will take over the Network when Carmine is gone."

Devanta signaled that the questioning was over. "I think we'd better take him down to the Knish place and wake him up."

Cannone's last words before waking up were "Something's up my ass."

Chapter 41

Andy sat in bed, propped up on two pillows in a convalescent center. He was alert and could move his arms and legs but couldn't yet walk. A wheelchair stood by the bed but he could barely manage to get into it by himself.

Claire entered and gave him a peck on the forehead. "How's it going Uncle Andy?"

Andy smiled, leaned forward to give her a kiss, and said, "Better every week. I still have trouble with my legs, but soon, they say I'll be able to walk with a walker. Then, I may be able to get out of this place, and get you off the hook of watching the business for me."

Claire welcomed the chance to commiserate with her old family friend. "Good. It's not much fun watching the store but I can't say it hasn't been interesting."

Andy worried about the "interesting" part. He turned his head to better read her facial expression. "Not too interesting, I hope. What's been so interesting?"

Claire shook her head, smiled back at him, and said, "We subtly questioned Lou Cannone about how things were going and got some disturbing answers. Are you up to hearing about it and maybe giving me some advice?"

"Bet your ass. What's up?" he replied, looking pleased.

Claire was torn. Should she give him the details and worry him, or should she go it alone? She decided. "Without going into the details of how we got him to talk, we learned that he sells hard drugs, and he sells them to kids. He's paying off Will Knap, probably to keep him quiet about the drugs, and if you don't know about these, he's probably got his hand in your till and is probably robbing you blind. And that's the good news. The bad news is that he can't wait for you to keel over so he can take over your business and, last, he said that someone's put a contract on Carmine's life."

Andy knew she had to be right but still wanted assurance. "Can you back up what you just said?"

Claire was glad to have others to corroborate this situation with Andy. "I'll bring you the three people who were with me. One of them was Mila. She tipped me off that something was brewing with Lou."

Andy knew what needed to be done. "He's my sister's kid. If what you say is true, he and his wife and kids will get new identities, a nice golf course in Florida to manage, and a check in the mail every semester for his kids to go to college. If he tries to give me any trouble, I'll have to deal with him differently."

Claire was reassured. "That's just what Carmine said you would do. He sends regards to your sister Sylvia."

Andy still looked troubled. "What do you think about what Lou said about Carmine?"

Claire replied, "I'm worried."

Chapter 42

NYU's Skirball Institute of Biomolecular Medicine on First Avenue and 23rd Street connects to the other buildings of the NYU Medical School Campus. Its twenty-five stories house research labs and spacious faculty offices.

It was the most magnificent medical structure that Devanta had ever seen. He entered a large corridor which was enclosed by glass windows and with huge columns supporting a very high ceiling. He was immediately greeted by a young woman who was, to his eyes, as glorious and well fashioned as the building. She welcomed him to the campus, hoped he had a good trip from India, and introduced herself as his guide for the day and as a graduate student in microbiology, the department that had arranged for his visit.

Her shoulder length blonde hair covered the collar of her white laboratory coat. He did not remember hearing her name but saw it embossed on the lab coat. Devanta surreptitiously tried to read the name, as she walked with him down the hallway, but her gait, and the gentle swaying of her bosom over which the name was written, made the task difficult. As soon as she recognized his plight, she stopped at a drinking fountain, and paused in her walk, giving him a moment to stop and gaze at the name, Andjelkovic Moland.

"My mother is Serbian and my Father was Norwegian, she said after she was certain he had read the name. Andjelkovic means 'little angel' in Serbian. Do you like it?"

Devanta was unable to respond. He was at once fascinated and disturbed by the soft voice, the speech with a hint of Middle European accent, and a face that matched her angelic name. For the first time he could remember, this highly successful forty year old university professor and former freedom fighter trained in martial arts, was rendered speechless by another human being.

Max Board, the Chairman of the Microbiology Department, greeted them in his office. He congratulated Devanta on his recent work and thanked him for coming to discuss it with the other members of the research community at NYU.

After lunch in the glittering, glass enclosed cafeteria, they walked together to the conference room where Devanta would give his talk. Fifteen PHDs, MDs, graduate students, and medical students rose in applause when Devanta was introduced.

Devanta described his new technology that allowed for isolation and analysis of all of the possible mutations of the RNA genetic makeup of the Staphylococcus aureus bacterium which could lead to its developing antibiotic resistance, and prevent curing the serious infections this organism could cause. He went over the history of penicillin, the first effective drug against Staph. "The earliest mutated strains of Staph which were resistant to penicillin secreted penicillinase, an enzyme that inactivated penicillin. New forms of penicillin were synthesized that were resistant to the penicillinase but Staph was resilient and battled back. New penicillins and other antibiotics were developed, but Staph quickly developed resistance to these in a never ending battle between the bacterium and the drugs developed to fight it. Finally, one drug, Vancomycin, had maintained its activity against most strains of Staph for almost a decade. But in recent years, more and more strains had become resistant to this drug, especially those strains that were acquired by hospitalized patients."

Devanta described how his new technique could be used to develop antibiotics to counter all mutations of the bacteria that could cause resistance.

Devanta then talked about his new drug, Vishnamycin which in early trials, was proving effective against strains of Staph aureus that were resistant to all other antibiotics.

After his talk, Devanta and Max chatted in Max's office. Max asked Devanta about the facilities that were available to him in India, and then described the office space, research space, and high tech equipment that were available at Skirball. Devanta knew that with these resources at his disposal, his work would be easier and would proceed more quickly. After lunch Max implied that there was always financial support from the Department for new faculty with important research projects until their grant proposals could be funded by the NIH.

After Devanta's meeting with the faculty, Andjelkovic returned to give him a tour of the Medical School building and the rent-subsidized residential units at the Skirball. The elevator from the residential units was packed with people. As he stood in front of her in the elevator, Devanta was conscious of Andjelkovic's presence behind him and felt the gentle pressure of her breast on his back. He was distracted and missed her telling him of her enthusiasm for his research. Andjelkovic was confident that Board was ready to offer him a faculty position. She also said that if he accepted, and wanted her to, she would be honored to work with him.

Chapter 43

Carmine was in his office taking the first bite of his peanut butter and jelly sandwich when the phone rang. "Hi Claire, what's up?"

Claire speedily pedaled her stationary bike. She slowed down a bit and asked, "Carmine, are you drunk, or are you eating?"

"I'm eating a sandwich."

There was little Claire enjoyed more than teasing her father, "Are you into the peanut butter and jelly again? Don't you know there are children starving all over the world who would love a PBJ?"

Carmine struggled to finish his second bite. "I'll send a case of each to whatever impoverished country you like. Just make sure I get some good publicity for it," he replied. "You can get some kudos yourself. Just tell them you got me to do it."

"I think I'd rather blackmail you. How'd you like the world to know that the head of the mob is a secret PBJ junkie?" and, not waiting for an answer, Claire continued, "I want to fill you in on the details of the meeting with our out of town guests. It'll be at our Network offices in the Freedom Tower."

"Good," said Carmine, "How will they get there?"

"I've rented suites for the guests at the Waldorf ," replied Claire, "Limos will pick up those who want transportation and deliver them to the meeting in time for lunch which will be at

Noon and will be catered by the Four Seasons restaurant. I don't think they have PBJs though."

Carmine finished the last of the sandwich, swallowed and said, "I'll try not to starve."

Claire continued, "I'm working on the agenda. We'll break at five PM and meet for Dinner at Papa Leone's. Iz arranged for us to have the restaurant to ourselves for the evening. OK?"

Carmine put the two jars in a desk drawer and the knife and plate in the trash. "Terrific! I wonder if Iz still has the tables bugged. I'll set up a Skype teleconference and let everyone know the plan."

That afternoon a large flat screen on the wall of the Network conference room displayed the faces of the twelve Network participants, all at their own locations. Each participant could see all of the others on similar screens at their office locations.

Carmine began, "OK, everybody's here. I just wanted to let you all know that we're on for the big meeting. Our prospective new partners are all supposed to be coming. We'll put 'em up in the Waldorf, feed 'em well, put on our best faces, and see what happens. Iz made Papa Leone's available for dinner at no cost to the Network. Mila will arrange for feminine companionship for those of our out of town guests who want it."

Jaime Poquito smiled, "We'll learn a lot from the bugs on the tables at Iz' place. Mila,where are you hiding **your** bugs?"

Mila was not to be upstaged, "I used to have them inserted in the girls' silicone implants, but with the new salt water implants, the bugs float around and make a racket during er (pause) exercise. Soon, they'll be making them small enough to put right next to the implantable birth control devices, so they will be harder to spot."

Chapter 44

Fiorella's personal phone rang in her office and Carmine's name appeared on its LCD. "Hi, Carmine. What's up?"

Carmine's voice was jocular as usual, but a bit tentative. "Fifi, good to hear your voice. I have something pretty delicate that we should go over. Could we meet in private, without a sea of reporters or any fanfare?"

"He's really worried," she thought, but replied, "What did you have in mind?"

Carmine sounded relieved: "Well, perhaps we could have a quiet chat at my place after you perform the ceremony."

Fiorella was amused and maybe a little hopeful. "Go to your apartment? Then what ceremony?"

Carmine hesitated, took a deep breath, "I was hoping you could marry Magda and me and then we could have a nice quiet discussion. And nobody would have to wonder what we were talking about. Mayors marry people all the time, don't they?"

All hope of fulfillment of her fantasized relationship with Carmine now gone, Fiorella wondered about the naivete of her friend. "So, let me understand what you're saying. You want to have a nice quiet chat with me and performing the marriage ceremony will be your cover?"

Carmine, astonished when confronted with the absurdity of his plan, said softly, "Well, sort of. Two fish on one line, you know."

Fiorella, her anger mounting over her evidently being the bottom fish on Carmine's line, replied, "Does Magda know about **how** you decided to get married?"

Carmine very quietly replied, "Not exactly. I haven't really asked her yet."

Fiorella, almost shouting, "He's patz!(crazy) And here I've been telling people how smart you are and how I'd love to have you on my ticket when I run for president. Now, I'd have to first convince myself that you're not nuts. Do me a favor. Ask Magda, and, if she's dumb enough to say yes, call me back."

A contrite Carmine replied, "Thanks. As usual, you're right Fifi."

Fiorella, half laughing, half crying mumbled, "Scooch!" (pest.)

Chapter 45

The March wind was cold on their backs as Claire and Carmine walked briskly down Fifth Avenue to Tiffany's at Fifty Seventh Street. Once inside, they were greeted by Louise Darkfield, who ushered them into a small simply but elegantly decorated room. Louise was in her forties, small and thin, and, like the room, simply but elegantly dressed. Her dark, shoulder length hair was tinged with gray. Her loose black turtle-neck sweater and small, pointed breasts caught Carmine's eye. She smiled as they wandered down to her black, wool skirt.

She ushered Carmine and Claire to two chairs at a small table and opened a black felt box where an array of a dozen diamonds rested on black velvet. The diamonds glistened in the light of a recessed overhead light shining directly on the table.

Louise looked at Claire, then at Carmine. "Mr. Cacciaguida, these are a small selection of clear, white diamonds, cut perfectly, in proportions to best refract light to give them maximum brilliance." and to Claire, "Are you the intended recipient?"

Claire twinkled, "No, I'm only the daughter. Besides, I would be too old for him anyway."

Louise, with just a hint of a smile, "I see," and to Carmine, "Do any of these interest you?"

Carmine enjoyed the moment but definitely needed help. "The one near the middle on the right. What do you think of that one Claire?"

"I guess that's about two and one quarter carats. Don't you think that's a little small for her?"

Carmine wondered for a moment if a bigger diamond wouldn't be better, but said "I don't know, Magda's just about the least materialistic person I know. I'm not sure she wouldn't be embarrassed to wear a bigger rock."

Claire got a kick out of how naïve her dad could be. "Carmine, in the company you keep, she would have the smallest rock. " I like this one," she said, rolling a large stone between her thumb and forefinger. It looks to be just over three carats."

"Just so," said Louise, "three and two tenths carats in fact, and an excellent choice. I suggest a simple Tiffany setting for now, and she can return with it to design a permanent setting, should she desire to do so."

As Claire removed a tissue from her bag and blew her nose, Louise said softly to Carmine, "Of course, you can return at any time if you want some personal attention, whether about diamonds or anything else, from someone a little closer to your age."

"I'll take it, the diamond. And thanks for the compliment."

Chapter 46

In the hallway outside Magda's apartment, Carmine could hear a recording of William Warfield singing "Bess, you is my woman now; you is, you is, and you must learn to sing and dance for two instead of one," from Gershwin's *Porgy and Bess*. A bunch of roses in his left hand, he rang the doorbell but his hands were sweaty. He had never proposed to anyone before. Bernice had proposed to him, which made things easy. Magda had talked about getting married but was she serious? She was, after all much younger than he, and she was remarkably bright and beautiful. Suddenly, his confidence vanished. Was he out of his mind? How could she say yes? The small box with the ring in his pocket now felt peculiar.

The door opened and there was Magda, a surprised look on her face. He hadn't called to let her know he was coming. She was even more surprised at the sight of the roses. In jeans and a sweater, with no make up, her face had an angelic glow. Carmine could hardly speak.

"Flowers! Who died? You don't have to answer; come on in. What a nice surprise, you, and the flowers."

Carmine was dazed, "You have a Southern accent."

"Some Yankee you are." Magda gently pulled him into her apartment. "You just noticed my accent? I'm from Texas and we've been together six months!"

Wistfully, "You look wonderful!"

"Wow, I'm not sure what's come over you, but I think I like it. Are you all right?"

"What are you doing Saturday night?"

"Well, I was fixin' to run off with Chuck Baillie from the Chicago gang. He has a nice line of American Moll dolls. I thought I would fit right into his lineup. Did you have something else in mind?"

Taking the ring from his pocket and offering it to her, "I thought we might get married, if Chuck Baillie doesn't mind."

"I don't know, Carmine, I have a mid-term exam in Near Eastern foreign policy on Monday; would you mind postponing it for a few weeks?"

"Is that a "Yes, you will marry me?"

"You bet it's a yes, and I'm just kidding about postponing it. We can do it tomorrow if you want!"

"I've got Fifi LaGuardia lined up for Saturday to do the ceremony. Is that OK?"

"I love you, and I'll gladly marry you but I can't help wondering why now? Why the sudden proposal?"

"I can't explain it but when we talked about me taking over for Andy, you were so strong, so loving, and so right, that I knew then I needed you with me forever. And, things look a little risky for me at the moment and I guess I want to be sure about the woman I love."

"Carmine, I think I like this. I like doing some mothering. But, you sure it's not that you might die living in sin and get turned away by Saint Peter at the pearly gates?"

The voice of Leontyne Price was singing "Porgy, I's your woman now, I is, I is, and I ain't never goin' nowhere lest you says so first."

Chapter 47

Dee's one bedroom apartment had only two reminders of home. One was a photo of her mother Mamaji, her father Dadiji, and her younger sister Vasanti which was on her bedroom wall; the other was one of Devavta which sat on her nightstand.

The bed next to the nightstand rocked with the rhythm of their lovemaking, pausing for a moment as each of the two partners came to climax, and then ceasing its motion. "Sorry for the squeaky bed," said Dee, "It came with the apartment."

"I've waited so long for this moment that I didn't even hear it." said Devanta, "I think of you every night. I remember your sweet face, your tender caresses, and the taste of every part of your body. I dream of never having to be separated from you, of waking up in the morning and having breakfast with you, of having kids with you."

He did not share with her his fantasy of doing the same with Andjelkovic.

The next morning, as he brushed his teeth, Dee stepped from the shower and reached for a towel. He gently caressed her.

"I could easily get used to this, Durgayoni. Being with you is never dull."

"I'm glad Devanta, because I love being with you, and because you could help a lot if you stayed a little longer to watch over Carmine for us. Word is that there is an assassin who is going to try to kill him at his big Network meeting. He's touchy about people looking as if they're guarding him. He likes to keep his 'Man of the People' image, which doesn't go well with bodyguards around him. So you'd have to keep a low profile. We wouldn't even tell him about you."

"What about my research and graduate students in Chandigarh? I can't put that on hold indefinitely."

"They can wait, but if they manage to kill Carmine, we'll never know if he could really have succeeded in controlling crime. Besides, I love being with you and I think we must learn if there is a future for us together," she lied.

"What do you want me to do?"

"I want you to be the big, strong, resourceful man I knew in India, the one who could use any means necessary to defend a principle, or a colleague in danger."

"OK. I suggest we start by visiting the Freedom Tower where Carmine works, and taking a look around. Then, maybe we can put on some running shoes and take a jog around the neighborhood. I have to get back into shape. You do have running shoes don't you?" Dee shook her head. "In that case, we'd better get you some. I hate to run alone."

Chapter 48

"Mr. Cacciaguida, I'm Richard Stone and this is Pete Stevens from Time Magazine. Pete will get some shots here in your home, and later a few in your office and one in the studio for the cover."

"Good enough. Nice to meet you gentlemen."

Carmine ushered the two men into the living room and offered them chairs. Pete preferred to wander around looking at the apartment and stopped in front of a painting of an old Basque woman that Carmine and Bernice had bought some years ago in Paris. "*Good*," Pete thought, as he continued looking for good backdrops for the photographs he would take.

"Mr. Cacciaguida," said Richard, "I'm fascinated by how you started this revolution in crime prevention. Have you heard of Malcolm Gladwell's *The Tipping Point?*"

"Yes. Why?"

"Gladwell talks about a tipping point where a revolutionary idea or a new trend or pattern of behavior really takes off. It takes a good idea, a few special people, and the right set of circumstances. The special people are a mayven, a salesman, and a connector. Which are you?"

"That's very flattering but this took a lot of hard work by some of the Network members who helped me get the others on board and by Claire, my daughter, who manages the Network."

"Is it true that you sold the idea to the Network members by packaging it as a form of protection?"

"It's little things that count, like packaging an idea so it appeals to all the parties that need to be convinced. To Congress, it was a novel cost effective plan to reduce crime and all its costs to society. To the mayor, the police, and the overworked court system, it was a means to reduce their workload and to have them appear more effective. I had to use other arguments with the Network. In the end, everybody wins."

Magda entered, wearing a skirt and a loose fitting, low-cut blouse, and carrying a tray of hors d'oeuvres, a pitcher of lemonade and some glasses. "Would you like a snack, gentlemen, or something to drink?"

"OK," said Richard, pouring himself some lemonade. "Mrs. Cacciaguida, what do you think of your husband's Network? Nice bunch of guys?"

"They're not all guys and they're not all so nice, but I prefer to think of what they've accomplished, like all the young kids who aren't going to jail or getting shot doing stickups, and all the people who aren't getting stuck up. All the women who still have their husbands. All the mothers who still have their kids. The new prisons that now won't have to be built. The cops, who don't have to work overtime and can spend time with their families, don't get burned out and shoot at anything that moves. Would you like some canapés, Richard?"

As Magda bent over the tray of hors d'oeuvres, she was briefly illuminated by a burst from the strobe light on Peter's rapidly clicking Nikon. Peter smiled, "With all respects, Mr. Cacciaguida, sir, she makes a much better picture than you do. But we'll do our best for you with the shots we take in the studio. Can I have a nice three quarter smile, Mrs. Cacciaguida?"

Richard Stone noted the Phi Beta Kappa key pinned on her blouse, the large diamond on her finger, the hint of a Texas twang in her voice, and her perfect face. "Where did you get the Phi Beta Kappa key, Mrs. Cacciaguida?"

"The University of Texas. I majored in math." She glanced at her finger and smiled affectionately. "The ring is from Carmine. We're not actually married yet; we're getting married next week."

Peter continued to pepper the room with his strobe light, although only occasionally was Carmine his subject.

Richard recovered from his surprise at her academic prowess. Still looking at Magda, "I'm told you're not as active at modeling as you once were. Has being an engaged woman changed your perspective on modeling?"

Magda grinned, "No, it's just that I have less time now that I'm a grad student."

Richard reached toward the coffee table, picked up a chocolate chip cookie. "What are you studying?"

"I'm working on my PhD. in Poly Sci. at Columbia. My thesis will be on the impact of the candidates' personal characteristics in the last four campaigns for the presidency. I'm working with my advisor on a new system to mine the data from media and other sources. In fact, I have a meeting scheduled with him in half an hour. So I hope you will all excuse me." And, to Carmine, "see you later hon." In seconds, she was gone.

Richard waited for Magda to leave and turned back to Carmine, "This is going to be a better piece than I thought. Not that you're not a story by yourself, Mr. Cacciaguida, but Mrs. Cacciaguida is quite a person in her own right. I'd have to check with my editor first, but would you mind if we had a picture of the two of you on the cover?"

Carmine grinned, "Just as long as you leave me in the picture, I'm OK with whatever you do. And, you can call me Carmine, most people do."

"Thanks." Richard frowned. "On a less happy note, is what you're doing dangerous? I mean, here you are, working with criminals to get rid of crime. Isn't someone going to want to bump you off?"

Carmine laughed. "You mean working with **other** criminals. To tell the truth, I feel safer than I did before managed crime. I have my first non bullet-proofed car. I don't run around with bodyguards. Besides, working with the Network is what I do and I gotta' do what I gotta' do.

Peter moved closer to Carmine. "Mr. Ca…Carmine, can I take one of you looking out the window, over the city?"

Chapter 49

Harlan Dreyfus entered through the revolving door into the broad lobby of the Freedom Tower. The metal detector beeped loudly, but Harlan's FBI identification, gained his passage past the guards at the entrance. He strode between the indoor ponds and waterfalls and took an express elevator to the Network offices on the eighty sixth floor.

The windows overlooking the view of lower Manhattan from Carmine's office were speckled by spattered rain drops. Carmine's outstretched hand and smile welcomed Harlan. "I hear you know my daughter Claire from college."

Carmine's handshake was firm and confident. "Yes sir, Mr. Cacciaguida, that's true. I used to sit a few rows behind her so she wouldn't notice my staring at her."

"Well," said Carmine, ushering Harlan into a chair. "You have good taste. Please call me Carmine; all of my friends do." Carmine ignored the chair behind his desk and pulled up another one to sit directly across from Harlan.

Harlan was delighted to finally meet Carmine. He was in awe of the man's celebrity. But his task that day was sobering. "All right then," he said, "Carmine it is. I'm certainly one of your admirers. But I'm here on business."

Carmine feigned anxiety, "Uh Oh! Are you going to give me a Miranda warning? Are we being recorded? Is the room bugged?"

Dreyfus shifted in his chair and sighed, "No, No, and maybe. I don't have to tell you that we share a common interest in the success of your business. Part of my job is to make sure nothing interferes with your success in reducing crime, especially something like your getting killed."

"Everybody is suddenly worried about my getting killed! I get the same thing from Claire. Why should I get killed? Us crooks are getting paid to do nothing, cops can play pinochle and eat free doughnuts without fear of interruption, courts have gotten over their huge dockets, and citizens can walk the streets without being mugged. Every body wins. So who would want to kill me?"

"We don't know but someone hired a killer in Malta. We've been tracking the killer's cell phone. The call we intercepted mentioned April thirteenth when you're having your meeting."

"You say in Malta. Milocchio's father, Rudolfo used a hit guy named Facciabrutta who took contracts over the telephone. Nobody ever saw him but he was good. As far as I know, he never failed. Not so good for me, is it?"

"We'll be looking for him but, as you've said, nobody knows what he looks like. Meanwhile, that call was placed from a cell phone between Seventy Third and Seventy Fourth Streets on Broadway. Know anyone who lives there?"

"Iz Milocchio lives in the Ansonia Apartments near there."

"I know that. Take a look at this." Harlan handed Carmine a piece of paper. On it were two identical fingerprints. "The one on the right is from the note handed to the teller in the second of the two robberies at the Dime Bank in Brooklyn. We had no match for it but after we tracked the cell phone call to the Ansonia, we pulled this off Milocchio's application to Yale Law School. It's good they don't throw these away. It's a perfect match."

Carmine sat motionless, trying to absorb the news.

Harlan continued. "This may sound unorthodox, but do you have a handgun?"

"Haven't had one in years. Never carry one. Didn't think I needed one."

Harlan opened his attaché case and removed a small black pistol. "Take this. And I advise you to keep it on your person and use it, if necessary. If you're questioned by anyone, here's a concealed weapon permit signed by my boss, William Cleaver, the Regional Director of the FBI in these parts."

"This has to be a first, the FBI arming a criminal."

"You're no criminal Carmine, at least not now."

"If I'm no criminal, how come everybody's paying me protection?"

"Carmine, if you're a criminal, how come I'm protecting you?"

Chapter 50

Mayor "Fifi" LaGuardia enjoyed her ride from Gracie Mansion to Carmine's apartment in the Trump Towers. From the back seat of the limo, she could rest for a few minutes and enjoy the views along the FDR Drive.

The view from Carmine's apartment was spectacular. She loved looking at New York City, her city. If it weren't for a hot flash or two, this would be a perfect day.

This was an intimate group of only six people in attendance: Carmine, Andy, his best man, in a wheel chair, Claire, and Magda's best friend Sarah from Texas, her maid of honor, Magda was somewhere in the apartment, but was waiting to make her grand entrance.

"When did Carmine stop calling her Limber?" Fifi wondered, *"That must just have been her nom de boob."*

She inquired, "Carmine, why so few people? Are you in hiding?"

"In a way," he replied, "maybe we'll talk about that after the ceremony, OK?"

"Sure hon, whatever you want. I know you have another agenda besides the triviality of getting married. Also, I guess this means it's time for me to stop waiting around for you to marry me. I'll just have to be satisfied to have you as my running mate."

"Fifi, I may jog a little, but I don't run. Where are you running to anyway?"

Andy wheeled over, having heard some of their repartee, and tossed in, "Left wing, right wing, west wing, just going to wing it?"

Claire approached, saying, "Magda's ready to come out now. Let's not keep her waiting. Andy, you're on." Andy removed a bright silver harmonica from his jacket pocket and began playing the Wedding March. All sang "Here comes the bride. Here comes" and Magda entered, in a fitted ivory, silk, knee length sleeveless gown with a high collar. A crown of baby's breath rested on her head. She was followed by Sarah.

"Never mind marrying you, "Fifi said, "I could forget about men and marry that!"

"Well," Carmine said, "you'll get the chance to marry us both, to each other."

"OK" declared Fifi, looks like we're all here; let's get to the marrying."

The service was brief, a few words of encouragement to the bride and groom from Fifi, an exchange of rings and vows, and they kissed. There were hugs all around.

"Fifi and I have a little business to take care of," Carmine, announced as he and Fifi moved into his study.

"OK, what's up Carmine? Are you going to get your picture on the cover of Time?"

"As a matter of fact, yes. They already came to interview me and take pictures, but I've got some information I think will interest you. It's sensitive."

"So, I'm sensitive to sensitive topics. Stop pussyfooting!" "OK, first, it looks like one of your cops is crooked. Lieutenant Will Knap of the 62nd precinct in Brooklyn is sabotaging us. He prevented a thorough investigation of the two recent bank heists in Bensonhurst, and he's being paid off by an unknown person in the Network."

"How'd you find out about Knap? We've had him under surveillance for the last month. We got a tip from one of his officers, a Hiroaki Nishiyama. We expect to bust Knapp pretty soon."

"I was tipped off by a former member of Andy's Bensonhurst provider group. He needs to remain nameless and is now thoroughly out of the picture."

"What else do you have on the bank robberies and murders?" she asked, not surprised that Carmine knew more about the crimes than she did.

"The FBI has a fingerprint on one of the notes handed to a teller during the second heist and they have a match for it but," he lied, "I don't know who it is."

Fifi spotted the lie but decided not to press the point. This couldn't be what's bothering Carmine. "What's the other part?" she asked. "It looks like someone may be trying to put a hit on me. I might have enemies after all-possibly someone in the Network. I'm not sure who it is."

"That's pretty sensitive! How can I help? I could assign some officers to protect you."

"I don't think that would work. We have a bunch of prospective Network members coming to town soon from all over the country. The last thing I need is to be surrounded by cops when they get here. Wouldn't be good for my image to look like I need protection and that I'm in bed with the cops. I'm planning to introduce the concept of managed crime to them but they're skeptical and wouldn't understand the cops. It's enough that Dreyfus, my own 'personal' FBI agent, knows about this. He was worried enough that he handed me a gun, complete with an FBI permit. I suspect he'll be having me watched. I don't think there's anything else you can do, but I wanted you to know."

Chapter 51

Carmine arose early on the morning of April thirteenth, the day of the big meeting. He promised Abe Bernstein that he would bring bialys to the meeting. So he planned to stop at Zabars's and pick some up on the way.

The bialy is a round onion roll with the consistency of pita bread which has a depressed central portion that is covered with pieces of onion. It was brought to the United States along with bagels, by Jews from Eastern Europe and is currently found mostly in New York City.

Carmine, dressed in a Zegna black pinstripe suit, pale blue Versace shirt, and striped Bugatti necktie, steered the Volt west on Fifty Sixth Street, and then north on Tenth Avenue. The top was down, it was sunny and in the sixties, and there were no birds overhead. It was a beautiful day to begin expanding the Network. He heard a clicking sound from behind the dash that he hadn't heard before and decided he'd get it looked at if it didn't go away.

He parked next to the "No Parking" sign on Broadway and eightieth, across the street from Zabar's. It was Good Friday, there was little traffic, and he could afford the ticket if he got one. Besides, he would only be inside for a few moments.

From the bakery/deli counter came the mingled odors of breads and rolls of all sorts. There was only one customer at the counter ahead of him, a short, stout, elderly woman with a babushka, a trace of mustache and a slightly balding scalp.

"From the middle, you should give me. The end of that lox is dried out. Also, only the pink, give me. The brown is feh!"

The clerk, with a white apron, knife poised over the lox and a smirk on his face, had endured similar requests dozens of times. "Only pink from the middle, I'll give you. Don't worry!" He cut off the end, tossed it into the trash, and began slicing the lox.

Adjusting her babushka, "And a small Whitefish, not too dried out."

"It's a smoked fish, lady. They all look dried out on the outside. The inside is deeelishious!"

"OK, and you got some salt bagels, but not too salty. My doctor says I shouldn't eat too much salt."

"Here lady, these are the salt bagels. Lots of salt!"

"Look at all that salt. I'm such a good customer and with salt, he wants to kill me! You got some with less salt maybe?"

"Lady, I got bagels with salt or I got bagels without salt. I don't got partly salted bagels."

"Bagels with no salt! Who would eat bagels, no salt? Feh! Give me four, with salt. The extra, I'll pick off."

"Lady, these are healthy bagels. Your doctor probably eats these by the dozen. God on high should strike me down if these are dangerous bagels."

They were deafened by a huge explosion and blinded by the glare of a ball of flame centered on the Volt, just outside, next to the "No Parking" sign.

"See?" said the babushka.

Chapter 52

Suddenly the hints and threats of his being in danger were real. *"The Volt would not blow up of its own accord"*. Someone was working hard to kill him. *"Marrone! I've got to get out of here."* As he turned to avoid the retreating babushka, he jostled a short man with a big moustache, wearing a blue blazer and holding a newspaper. With a polite nod of apology, he made for the first of the four large exits from Zabar's and groped for his mobile phone. *"No phone. Manage la miseria! Left it at home! Who in hell would want to kill me? Worry about that later. Got to stay alive. Got to get to the meeting."*

With his mind racing, Carmine walked briskly looking for a cab. He saw one across the street but the woman with the babushka was at the door, about to get in. He raced over to the cab with a twenty dollar bill in his hand to pay her to allow him to use the cab but he was too late. The cab sped off before he could get there. He walked quickly for one block where a number 104 bus heading downtown was picking up passengers. He hadn't taken a bus in several years but the bus, with one transfer, would take him to the Freedom Tower and his meeting.

"Say Bud, you need a Metro Card to get on this bus."

"I'm sorry but this is an emergency. That's my car burning on Eightieth Street. I've got to get downtown and I don't have a card." Reaching into his pocket and removing the twenty dollar bill, "Will this cover the cost? You can keep the change." "OK, Bud, I believe you, so have a seat but keep the money. No charge this time."

Carmine took a seat at the front of the bus. His Versace shirt was drenched in sweat and stuck to his chest. He removed his suit jacket and took a deep breath.

The Asian man to his left was carrying a book. Carmine leaned over to read the title *English/Tibetan*. Across from him was a group of men speaking Hebrew. The bus stopped at Sixty Third Street and picked up more passengers, a mother and her young son both speaking Spanish. She wore a sweatshirt with the word Rensselaer on the front. Carmine's eyes followed them until they found seats. They sat down next to a man, a short man with a mustache and wearing a blue blazer. The man from inside Zabar's had followed him.

The next stop for the bus was on Forty Second Street. Carmine waited for the last passenger to get on board, and before the front door could close, he dashed out of it onto the Street.

He moved fast at Times Square. Good place to lose someone who could be following you, lots of people. Where's a cab? No cab. On the southwest corner of Broadway and Forty Second Street was a Tuck's men's clothing store. Carmine paused in front, turned, did not see the man in the blue blazer, and ducked inside. He took a gray sweatshirt and a pair of tan chino pants off the shelves and slipped into the dressing room. He hurriedly removed his Zegna suit, tie, and shirt, pulled the belt from his pants and put it on the chinos. He left his expensive clothing in the dressing room and emerged to hear the eleven AM news from a radio at the counter. "We have just learned that an exotic car owned by Mr. Carmine Cacciaguida, noted New York City managed crime organizer, has exploded at Broadway and eightieth Street. No further details are available at the moment as to the cause of the blast or the fate and whereabouts of Mr. Cacciaguida. Now we return to the ..."

Carmine gave a fifty dollar bill to the clerk." I'll take the sweatshirt and pants. Can I use your phone for a minute? It's an emergency."

"You look familiar to me. Did you ever teach at N.Y.U.? I know I've seen your face somewhere."

"People are always saying that to me .I must look like a lot of people. I really need to use your phone. Here's another twenty dollars. Will that cover the cost?"

Handing him the telephone, "Thanks. Sure, use the phone."

Carmine moved to the back of the store and dialed Claire's mobile phone but got her voicemail. "Claire, honey," he said quietly, "I'm leaving you this message to say that I'm all right. I don't know who blew up the car but I wouldn't be surprised if it turned out to be Milocchio. Remenber, the call to Facciabrutta was traced to the Ansonia. Also, Milocchio's fingerprint was on the note given to the teller in the bank robbery in Brooklyn. I'll be at the meeting but I may be a few minutes late. Have everybody wait for me. And, please call Magda and tell her I'm OK. I have to run, literally. Love you."

Carmine exited the store and passed a window-shopping dark skinned man wearing a tan, worn jacket, and with the worst pock marked face Carmine had ever seen.

Chapter 53

Claire went immediately to the Ansonia. "Iz, sorry to come over unannounced, but someone tried to kill Carmine!" she gasped, "They blew up his car! Fortunately, he wasn't in it. I'm so scared. I want to be with someone strong. I need to be with you for a little while until I can calm down. We can go to the Network meeting together. I promise I won't make you late. Just hold me."

Milocchio took her in his arms," I'm flattered. I don't usually think of myself as being the nurturing type, but under the circumstances, I'll do what I can. I can even play strong and silent if you like. Besides, it's been a while since you came over. I'd begun to wonder if you were losing interest in me."

Looking up into his face, "No, it's just been tight, with my two jobs. I haven't forgotten you. I'm glad you missed me."

Holding her tenderly, "I've missed holding you, and being close, like this."

Claire held him tighter. "I'm sorry. Let me make it up to you." She removed her coat, revealing only a teddy underneath. She moved with him to the bedroom. Her breasts were small under the teddy and her erect nipples stared out at him. Her neck curved as she bent to pull the two hairpins from her head, allowing her dark hair to fall gently to her shoulders. She put the hairpins on the nightstand and motioned him to move closer to where she sat on the bed. She slowly undid the knot of his tie and slid it off. Iz undid his top shirt button and she unbuttoned the next. Her hands moved to his belt buckle and opened it. Slowly, she unzipped his pants and smiled as she felt the rigid penis. He wriggled to allow his pants to fall to the floor. He reached to remove the teddy but she signaled him to wait. She drew him down on the bed and, still sitting, removed his undershirt. She motioned for him to pull down his shorts and she pulled off the straps of her teddy revealing her pink breasts, moving as she breathed. She rose, and facing him, straddled him and pressed against him, gently guiding him into her. Their rhythm was varied with her brief moments of holding her breath and then groaning until she gasped and was still. Iz held his breath, felt his climax begin, and then felt pain in the center of his chest. Claire pulled the thin ceramic stiletto from his heart and back out through the small hole it had made in the skin under his breastbone. Each heart beat now pumped blood out of the hole in his left ventricle, into the pericardial sac surrounding the heart. He felt pain, then nausea, and then weakness. In a few more beats, the pressure of the blood forced by the beats of his heart into the pericardial sac increased, the heart could no longer expand to fill with blood, and was no longer an effective pump. He felt surprised, angry, short of breath, and then, he felt nothing.

Claire was surprised at how little blood leaked from the wound. She wiped the blood off the stiletto with a tissue, flushed the tissue down the toilet, rinsed the stiletto in the bathroom sink and replaced it in the wooden scabbard that was her hairpin. She silently thanked Carmine for this set of special hairpins, her most important sixteenth birthday gift from her father, and to "uncle" Andy who had instructed her in their proper use, "under the breastbone, upwards toward the heart, ten degrees left and twenty degrees inward." She was surprised at the time, not that Andy knew how to use it, but that he could explain it in geometric terms. She was fifteen when she was raped. Her attacker, a young acquaintance, disappeared soon after, but her fear did not. She had been determined to be in control of her body ever since.

Although Claire's sexual partners were numerous and varied, the sex varied very little, and Claire was always in control.

She showered, removed undergarments and a dress from her handbag, got dressed rapidly, put on the red wig and large sunglasses she had worn when she entered the building, and headed for the Freedom Tower hoping to find Carmine there, alive.

Chapter 54

In his new hooded sweatshirt, Carmine at first felt anonymous and secure. He jogged down a subway staircase at Broadway and Forty First Street and took a Red Line, Number 2 train downtown. An accordion player with a tin cup walked from one end of the car to the other, playing *"Besame Mucho"* and got off at the next stop with no additions to his cup. Three teenage girls with shaved heads but dressed in pressed suits, neckties, sandals, and painted toenails discussed their mothers' ugly faded tattoos and questioned why their mothers put those ugly designs all over their bodies.

Carmine wondered when the train would get to Cortlandt Street, the stop for the Freedom Tower. *The train was heading into sunlight. It was on a bridge. What bridge? They were heading for Brooklyn. Must have passed Cortlandt Street!*

At the next subway stop, Carmine got off the train, headed upstairs and then downstairs to the uptown track, and got on the first uptown train that would get him to the Cortlandt Street station. A dark skinned blind man entered the subway car through the doors from the car behind, walked the length of the car, and left through the front door and into the next car. To his horror, Carmine recognized the worn-looking tan jacket, and around the dark glasses, the pockmarked face of the man at Tuck's Store on Times Square.

Carmine realized the train had reached Thirty Fourth Street. Again he had missed his stop. He rushed out of the train up the stairs, past an obese elderly woman struggling to pull a shopping cart filled with plastic bags, (her worldly possessions?) up the stairs. He saw no one behind him but his hooded sweatshirt impaired his peripheral vision."

At the top of the staircase was a maze of pathways and tunnels with signs for Red, Yellow, Orange, and Green Line trains. Carmine headed through a walkway marked Penn Station /Madison Square Garden. He counted four passed-out homeless men lying dead? alive? against the sides of the tunnel. An upward stairway led to the Manhattan Mall. Carmine scurried up the stairway into a three story shopping mall. He pulled down the hood of the sweatshirt and took a good look around. No dark skinned man with a pockmarked face in sight.

On the second floor of the mall was another Men's Shop. "Time to get rid of the sweatshirt," he decided. He entered the shop and emerged in a dark green Hawaiian shirt and sunglasses.

Still nobody in sight. He determined to find a cab and finally found one in front of Macy's Department Store on Thirty Second Street and Sixth Avenue. He directed the driver to the Freedom Tower. All of his suits except the Zegna had been tailor made. Now, he would face his colleagues in a green Hawaiian shirt. His Rolex clicked to eleven forty AM. He got to the Freedom Tower safely.

Chapter 55

Carmine was struck by the beauty of the Freedom Tower at the heart of the new World Trade Center. It had grown from a large hole in the ground, surrounded by empty space and partly destroyed adjacent buildings, to a magnificent spiral seventeen hundred seventy six-foot-tall glass-covered building.

The Network's Headquarters had moved in thirteen months earlier, after signing its first managed crime contracts. The three main entrances to the Tower were heavily guarded and all who entered had to pass through a metal detector. The entrances were in plain view from the adjacent buildings, and, Carmine knew, would make excellent spots for a marksman who might be interested in killing him. The least conspicuous entrance was a small loading dock to which all deliveries were made. A metal detector at the entrance was presided over by "Julio the Cardinal," who was aptly named for his prominent beak of a nose and his bright red jacket, sweater, and trousers. Julio, impressed by Carmine's celebrity status, warm salutations, and generous Christmas gifts, didn't bother to search Carmine in the past, when he set off the alarm and didn't search him this time either as he inquired about Julio's son who had just been accepted to law school at Columbia.

There were three banks of elevators, but only one reached the eighty sixth floor. Carmine headed for that one as he entered the lobby. To his relief, an armed, uniformed Tower security guard also approached the elevator. The guard entered the elevator first and moved to the back. Carmine followed, grateful for the added security of the guard. As the elevator doors began to close, two hands spread them open from the outside. One of the hands belonged to a sweating, out-of-breath man wearing a blue blazer and a large moustache. The other hand belonged to a dark skinned man with a pockmarked face, also sweaty and out-of-breath, who rushed in immediately afterwards.

The doors closed.

Wayne Wax fondled his moustache nervously with his left hand, his right hand touching the "thirty eight" in the jacket of his blue blazer, while inspecting the dark skinned man intently.

Devanta Singh worried about the man with the moustache. Could that be a gun in his pocket?

Facciabrutta fondled the garrote in his security guard's uniform pocket. This would have been the weapon of choice were it not for the two interlopers. Now he'd have to use his pistol and kill them all.

Chapter 56

In the cab, Claire removed the cell phone from her purse, and dialed. "Dee, glad you're there. …….."

At the Freedom Tower building, Claire passed the row of stylish, expensive, Chinese-made Vexus Limos hired to bring the out-of-town guests to the meeting. Cripes! They were already here and she hadn't been here to greet them.

As she entered the meeting room, she saw that all of the Network members were there except Carmine, Andy, and, of course, Iz. Abe Bernstein was picking through the bagels, looking without success for bialys.

Miguel from Houston and Baillie from Chicago were catching up on old times. Blake from Atlanta was chatting with Nat Bart who approached Claire as soon as she entered the room.

Nat enjoyed looking at her but enjoyed teasing her even more. "Pussycat, where's Papa Carmine? We need to start the festivities."

Claire replied, "He's going to be a little late. He called me and said he had car trouble."

Nat was not fooled. "Car trouble? I bet he had trouble getting past the big fire on Eightieth Street. That really backed up traffic."

Claire looked at him and stage whispered. "Don't be too disappointed when he shows up in a few minutes. I wonder what's happened to Iz? He's pretty meticulous about being on time, and where's Andy?"

Nat said to her rapidly retreating form, "I wouldn't worry too much about Milocchio. He's got his head screwed on tight."

Claire, still moving away from him whispered, "Try to hold the fort Nat, while I go look for Carmine." She left the room and headed for the elevator.

Devanta Singh's eyes were fixed on the object in Wayne Wax's pocket which he was sure was a gun. He decided not to take any chances with Carmine's life and, with all his force, he directed a fierce kick at the hand and the gun but, being long out of practice with his martial arts, instead hit Wayne squarely in the groin. Wayne crumpled in pain. Devanta, from the force of the kick, lost his balance and tumbled on top of Wayne as the elevator stopped to admit an old lady in a black dress and black lace shawl seated in a motorized wheelchair.

Carmine was staring at the two people on the floor of the elevator.

Facciabrutta put the garrote back in his pocket and reached for his pistol.

The old lady in the mechanized wheelchair pushed the joystick forward to turn up the speed, circled the two men on the floor and rammed the metal foot holders at the front of the wheel chair into Facciabrutta's legs, pinning him to the elevator wall with a loud crunch. Carmine was stunned. The "old woman" was Andy!

In a fluid motion, Facciabrutta, pulled out his gun and aimed it at Carmine in time to see Carmine's black pistol pointed at him.

A shot rang out and the elevator filled with smoke.

Chapter 57

As Claire reached the elevator, she heard the shot from the elevator shaft below. In a few seconds, the door opened to the smell of exploded gunpowder and Carmine emerged, a pistol in his hand, followed by Devanta and Wayne.

Facciabrutta was holding his painful left chest and was not able to put weight on his painful, seemingly broken left leg.

Carmine, Claire and Andy headed for the boardroom.

Wayne stood, one hand on his groin and the other with his gun pointed squarely at Facciabrutta. Devanta helped Facciabrutta off the floor of the elevator and into the hallway. Facciabrutta could stand only on one leg and held the other off the ground. He held onto Devanta's shoulder with his left hand and clutched his wounded chest with the other. Facciabrutta begged for them to let him use the men's room just across from where they stood. "Got to sheet! Got to sheet bad! Please? Please!"

The men's room had a row of five stalls on the left, and a row of urinals on the right. With Wayne's gun still pointed at him, Facciabrutta hopped into the men's room and entered the middle stall. Wayne and Devanta followed on his heels. Facciabrutta closed the door to the stall and sat on the toilet. Appropriate noises and a faint fecal scent arose from the stall. Wayne's gaze was fixed on the trouser legs resting on the pair of shoes on the floor of the stall, in front of the toilet. He used his cell phone to call Dreyfus with his news.

A teenaged boy emerged from the fifth stall, washed and dried his hands, and left. Shortly thereafter, the first stall toilet flushed, and a bearded man in a Comcast shirt and chino pants walked out of the stall and left without washing his hands. Devanta, always scrupulous about his personal hygiene, was appalled and had to restrain himself from upbraiding the Comcast man for not washing up after using the toilet.

But the shoes and trouser legs on the floor of Facciabrutta's middle stall remained motionless.

Wayne called out "Schmuck, it's enough time for you to have sheet twice. Get out of there!"

No answer.

"OK, I'm coming in after you." And without more waiting, Wayne kicked in the door.

He and Devanta stared at the shoes and trousers on the floor, and at the security guard jacket, shirt, and tie hanging on a hook on the inner side of the door. The jacket was padded with heavy material and lined with Kevlar. Under the hole on its right side was a bullet, lodged in the reinforced lining. There was a small amount of blood on the inner surface of one trouser leg. Urine and feces were in the toilet. But there was no Facciabrutta.

Later on, they would find a false beard in one of the two elevators that served the lower floors of the building.

Chapter 58

A bronze-skinned woman pushed a large linen cart through the hallways of the Ansonia to Iz's apartment on the sixth floor. She unlocked the door, cleaned the apartment, changed the bed linen with an identical white set, and when she emerged, the laundry basket was unusually full and heavy.

A few minutes later, a large flat screen high definition television was delivered to an apartment on the third floor of the building. Not long after, the carton from the TV left the building and was delivered to a Transafata Gigapizza. It was dropped off by a dark skinned man with a French accent and it was incinerated, along with its contents later that evening. The furnaces of the pizzeria were given their usual thorough monthly cleaning the next day.

As Carmine, Andy and Claire entered the meeting room, they were met by four of their out-of-town guests who were hurriedly heading out the door towards the elevators. Mohammed and Miguel were holding the elevator door while Phil was shouting at Carmine, "Why'd y'all have to pick today to get shot at? Cops'l be all ovah the place any minute. And where the hell is Milocchio? I'm getting mah ass out of here but I need to talk with you. Ah'll call you." And as he entered the elevator, "Knew Ah shouldn't have come here with all these yankees." The elevator door closed.

A moment later, when the police arrived, Abe Bernstein was munching on a chopped liver sandwich chiding Carmine about the missing bialys, smiling and saying, "It's good to be retired."

Chapter 59

The Saturday New York Times article was titled. "Cacciaguida Attacked in Elevator after his Car Explodes." Below that was "Vice President of Network is missing."

The New York Post headline ran "Crime Boss shoots attacker in elevator." And underneath, a smaller headline ran "VP of Crime network disappears. A hit gone wrong?"

Two weeks later, Harlan Dreyfus, Wayne Wax, and Bill Cleaver met in Cleaver's office to review their investigations on the attempted murder of Carmine and the disappearance of Milocchio. There was not much progress in either investigation.

As for the assassin in the elevator, they had an unhelpful description of a man of ordinary height and weight, with brown eyes and brown hair who sometimes wore a false beard. The DNA from the blood on his pants and the clumps of skin cells on the adhesive of the false beard would be helpful in identifying a suspect if and when they had one, but it matched no one in any of the U.S. or Interpol DNA databases. There were no complete fingerprints on the assailant's Glock 30SF.45 ACP subcompact pistol but there were some minute blue cotton fibers on the handle. The assassin must have wiped it clean with his uniform while he was on the elevator floor. A smudged incomplete print from his right index finger was present on the trigger. There were security camera videos of a man in a security guard's uniform in the lobby and entering the elevator but in all of them, his face was pointed away from the camera, as if he knew where the cameras were hidden.

The Malta airport was being watched for persons matching the assassin's description and several males had been stopped and questioned but the assassin was not identified.

Milocchio's whereabouts were still unknown. A thorough search of his apartment, the rest of the building, the Network central offices, his known hangouts, and each of the individual Network chief's central offices produced no sign of him. A search of the paths he frequented in Central Park was fruitless.

Carmine was questioned by the police and the FBI. He stated that he had no knowledge of the whereabouts of Iz Milocchio or what became of him. He, surprisingly to some, also denied ever having shot at anyone other than his assailant in the elevator, and denied ever having killed anyone. A polygraph test confirmed his statements.

The only finding of interest was a single speck of dried blood on the tiled bathroom floor of Milocchio's apartment, which proved on DNA testing, to be his blood.

"I suspect," said Harlan, "that Milocchio's gone, either dead or in hiding, but probably dead."

Wayne mused, "So either somebody wanted to knock off the two top Network leaders or there was a power struggle between Carmine and Milocchio, and Carmine won."

"Or maybe," Cleaver chimed in, "this fiasco was organized from someone else in the Network or by the group of thugs Carmine was going to meet."

"One thing we found could mean something." said Harlan, "A number on Milocchio's mobile phone. It's Phil Blake's. He's the mob guy from Atlanta. We questioned him in his hotel room after the aborted meeting. In the last two months, there were more than a dozen calls involving Phil Blake and Milocchio. Of course, Blake denies any involvement in either Carmine's attempted murder or Milocchio's disappearance. I think we should watch Blake."

In mid-May, Phil Blake called Carmine. "Y'all still freezin' up there in New York? It's nice and warm here in Atlanta."

Carmine replied "It was plenty hot here a few weeks ago but it's cooled down since then. Seems it was too hot for you to stick around here last month. Why'd you leave in such a hurry?"

"I'm allergic to cops. I get hooves when they get too close."

"You mean hives?"

"I mean hooves; helps getting away. But that's not the reason I'm callin' you. I'm thinking about joining your Network. How about we all meet on neutral turf somewhere?"

Carmine dialed Harlan's number. "Harlan, got a minute?...."

Harlan couriered a small package to Carmine.

Chapter 60

Sam Testabuona was bothered by the image of Bidetto Passalacqua's crusher converting the red Chevy Caprice into a flat piece of junk. *"Was this the Caprice used in the Dime Bank robbery? Where was Bidetto now and who was he working for?"*

Andy was relieved to finally get some information on Bidetto and asked Sam to work full time on finding him.

Sam hung out for a while with the workers in Poquito's chop shop and learned that Bidetto was in Georgia and working for a new boss. The only mob there of any significance was Phil Blake's.

Chapter 61

Synn's was the newest and most luxurious casino in Las Vegas. Carmine was greeted at the entrance and escorted to his suite by a pretty young blonde woman in a black pinstripe business suit. She assured him that he was a guest of the house and didn't need to register. She told Carmine that Mr. Blake would probably be at the slots. The furnishings in Carmine's suite were opulent.

Carmine headed down to the gaming room looking for Phil Blake who was perched on a seat in the middle of the first row of slot machines closest to the entrance to the room. Phil saw Carmine and grumbled. "A guy comes up to me, winks, and says for me to sit at this machine today. Every day they set some machines to be heavy winners. They stick shills at these machines. So the suckers hear lots of noise, see people winning and coins jingling and can't wait to sit at all the other machines set to deliver only a screwing. There they throw their kids' college educations into these toilets."

Blake quickly turned his gaze to his mounting pile of coins, and pulled down the handle. "Flush." he growled.

Carmine noted the beads of sweat on Phil's brow and said, "You seem to be doing OK."

"Sure," said Phil, "but they're not taking chances. The bastards gave me a good machine but it only takes quarters. They must be worried I'll break the bank." He dumped his winnings into a white plastic bag and stepped away from the machine.

"I hope our meeting will be a little more private than our last almost meeting in New York." Carmine said. Neither of them noticed the man with a large mole on his nose, who replaced Phil at the slot machine.

"Y'all can bet your Versaci boots it will be more private. No shooting and no cops." Phil weaved Carmine through the rows of machines into an elevator marked "Employees only," and into a locker room.

"OK, hot tub time," said Phil.

Both men hung their clothing in adjoining lockers and put on plaid trunks. Then Phil led them to a small room and into a hot tub with six noisy jets of bubbly water.

"Now that we all are relaxed, I'll tell you what's on my mind. I wasn't happy with y'all's Network at first but the more I think about it, the more I like its possibilities."

"I'm glad to hear it," said Carmine, I'd like to start thinking about how we could work out the arrangements. Did you have something in mind Phil?"

Phil scratched an itch on his great toe, turned to Carmine and casually rejoined, "I thought y'all might like to be governor of New York State."

Two attractive women appeared at the hot tub right after Blake's offer to Carmine. They removed their clothing while Phil smiled at them and Carmine hastily removed himself from the tub and from the room, shouting to Blake over the noise of the bubbling water, "I'm forty seven and a newlywed. I've got to conserve my energy for Magda." That's what he said, but he thought, *The last thing I need as a candidate for governor is a sneak picture of me in a hot tub with two naked women.*

Chapter 62

It was Wednesday and Claire was at Bloomie's trying on a beige suit when she saw the unmistakable figure of Harlan Dreyfus in the mirror, standing behind her. "If you're going to sneak up on me, it'll cost you at least another teddy."

"Not this time. I've been all over Bloomie's trying to find you."

Claire turned to face him. "So, remember what I said. Only business between us for now."

"Right," said Harlan, as he scrutinized the suit. "And it's important business."

Claire walked with him to a quiet spot. "What's up, Harlan?"

"The surveillance recording from the entrance to the Ansonia on the day Iz Milocchio disappeared showed a woman about your size with a wig and sun glasses entering and then leaving a half hour later just before the big Network meeting that Milocchio never got to."

"Surely you don't think I could have something to do with Iz disappearing, do you?"

"I would feel much better if you would answer some questions for us, preferably with a polygraph."

Claire looked down at the floor, thought for almost a minute and then looked directly into Harlan's eyes and replied, "I'm not interested in having you dig into all of my business Harlan. But if it will reassure you, I would be willing to answer these three questions and only these three questions with a lie detector. One: Did I kill Iz Milocchio? Two: How did he die? And three: Do I know anyone else who might have killed him? Would that do Harlan?"

"If that's what you're willing to give me, that's what I'll take, for now."

Chapter 63

That evening, Carmine sat with Magda sharing some details of his meeting with Blake. "Phil said that Senator Strong is a good friend and that he could broker a deal with Strong to get me nominated for Governor of New York on the Democratic ticket. In return, Strong would get to "help me decide on" appointments to some key positions in my administration. Strong also believes I would be well funded and that we could campaign together and 'assist each other's campaigns financially.' In other words, he would expect to get some financial backing from us. Blake says Strong thinks I would have a good chance of being elected."

Magda couldn't conceal her enthusiasm that Carmine could be Governor of New York. "So it would cost a little money and some patronage. That's not that unusual, I suppose. What are you going to do?"

Carmine didn't feel comfortable with this advice. The next morning he discussed Blake's offer with Claire. Claire's eyes widened, "You mean a month ago he told you that you were nuts, a couple of weeks ago he may have been the one who tried to arrange to get you killed, and now he's your buddy? You're not buying this BS, I hope!"

That afternoon, Carmine told Andy about the offer and about the two women at the hot tub.

Andy was blunt, "What does that cetriole want from you? I'd fuck him before he fucks you."

Chapter 64

The next week, Phil Blake "just happened to be in New York City on business" and arranged a follow up meeting with Carmine. They met at Carmine's Family Restaurant in the Theater District. Carmine's was always crowded and noisy but the owner enjoyed his namesake celebrity customer being there and always came up with a table for him without a reservation and without a wait.

Carmine and Phil were examining their menus when a small finger tapped Carmine on the shoulder. "Mr. Cacciaguida," came a high pitched child's voice from behind the finger. "My Mom said I should come over here and ask you to sign this menu."

"What's your name, big fella?"

"My name is Carmine, just like you, Carmine Falacci."

"And so is the name of this restaurant," added the older Carmine. He signed the menu and rose, walked over to the child's parents and congratulated them on their charming son.

When he returned, Phil patted him on the back, "A budding politician! I knew it! I couldn't do it. I would kiss the mammas, not the babies."

A waiter arrived with a large bowl of gnocchi. "The boss said the gnocchi is real good today. This is to start you off, compliments of Carmine's."

Phil laughed out loud and said, "See how nice they are to us? They must know who I am even in New York."

"I told them you were coming," Carmine teased, "I asked them to butter you up."

Phil turned serious. "So what do y'all think of my idea, the governor bit?"

"I understand about sharing the patronage and campaign funds with Strong but there's gotta' be more to it than that. What do you want out of this deal, Phil?"

"Like I said, it has to be good for our managed crime business to have one of us in a powerful place, good for signing up more insurance companies and more employers, and all around good for deals to increase our Network's reimbursement."

"That part seems good. What about other ways to increase our business? What about extending the types of crime we cover? How about hard drugs?" asked Carmine.

"Well," said Phil, "Y'all are right. We need to grow. I'd like to see us all over the U.S. Grow like hell! But we don't need to get rid of drugs! We need to go slow on that cash cow. Maybe hold the fort for a few years. Think about if we could afford it. Go very slow. It'll be fine, y'all will see."

"*So that's the hitch,*" thought Carmine, "*I would have to lay off controlling hard drugs. Andy was right.*"

"I'll think about it." responded Carmine. He said little and seemed busy with the gnocchi and the veal parmesan which followed. They agreed to meet again the following week.

Chapter 65

Sam Testabuona turned to his computer to track down Passalacqua. Google took Sam to www.gangsters.org which described Bidetto Passalacqua as a thief who tried unsuccessfully to rob banks. Bidetto had served a total of six years in penitentiaries in New York State.

Clipping service.com yielded several newspaper articles that cited Bidetto as a suspect in numerous thefts.

Wickepedia described Passalacqua as an altar boy, an Eagle Scout, valedictorian of his high school graduating class, and a businessman who supported numerous charities. There was no mention of penitence or penitentiaries.

None of the twenty six Google citations was helpful in finding Bidetto's current whereabouts.

Yahoo People search was more helpful. There was one Bidetto Passalacqua and one Theresa Passalacqua in Atlanta.

Sam flew to Atlanta and went to the first address, a nursing home, and found that this Bidetto was Bidetto Passalacqua Sr. who was eighty nine years old. Sam found the old man seated on the porch, eyes closed, enjoying the sunlight. "Com'esta? asked Sam, who thought it best to speak to the old man in Italian. The senior Passalacqua smiled and replied with no evident emotion, "Va mori ammazzato. Che ti passano mangia i bicimori!" (Go get killed. And may the worms eat your remains!) He had no more to say.

Repeated knocks on the open door of Theresa Passalacqua's home elicited no reply. "Anyone home?" Sam tentatively entered and found a teen age boy perched in front of a computer screen playing "Virgins and Whores." The object of the game was either to seduce virgins and save the whores or vice versa; Sam couldn't tell.

The teen manipulated the joystick with his left hand while his right hand picked a pimple on his chin. There was at first, no reply to Sam's greeting and no acknowledgement of his presence in the room.

"Hello," said Sam, "Do you know a Bidetto Passalacqua and where he might be?"

Without turning to see his questioner, the youth, said "Uncle B. lives around the corner, over the grocery store," and he wiped his thumb and forefinger on his jeans.

Sam made two quick phone calls, to Andy, and to Dreyfus' mobile phone.

As Sam dialed Dreyfus, Carmine stepped into the Delta Airlines Jet headed for Atlanta. Aboard the plane, Carmine turned off his mobile phone as instructed by the cabin crew.

Phil Blake had suggested that this time, the meeting should be at his headquarters in Atlanta. Carmine was still hoping that Phil could be convinced to join the Network. The prospect of running for governor seemed unlikely.

At about the time of Carmine's scheduled take off, the pilot's voice announced that there was a glitch in the plane's computer and that technicians had been called to try to fix it. It would be another hour before they would know if the problem could be solved. Carmine decided to take a nap while they waited.

Dreyfus' voice on Claire's phone sounded urgent. "Claire, Where's Carmine? I need to speak with him right away."

"He left for Atlanta this morning. You can try to get him on his mobile if he remembered to plug it in last night."

"That's not so hot. Bidetto Passalacqua was picked up by the Atlanta PD last evening. I got a tip about where he was staying, called the Atlanta (FBI) office and they arrested him. The amazing thing was that he seemed glad to see them. He had his bags packed and looked as if he was ready to get out of there in a hurry but he wasn't running from us."

"Why should he be running from you? I could understand it if you were chasing him around Bloomingdale's!"

"Claire, not now! No time for games. Carmine's in trouble. Passalacqua said that Blake was in on the hit on Carmine in New York City. He thinks Blake still might want to kill Carmine. I've got to find Carmine right away. I'll try to call him on his cell."

An hour later, Carmine was awakened by the pilot's voice saying that the technicians were still trying to fix the computer and it would be another forty five minutes before they would know if they could take off.

Carmine turned on his mobile phone and alerted Phil Blake that he would probably be late for their meeting. Phil said not to worry. They would hold the meeting when Carmine got there. Carmine again turned off his phone.

Dreyfus' voice was now urgent. "Claire, I can't get him on the phone. I need to find him right away. Are you sure he went to Atlanta? I asked him to call me every time he goes there and he hasn't called me."

"He told me last evening that he was going there first thing this morning. There's no plane out of New York City now until late this afternoon. If you need to get to him right away, I can take you. Meet me at Teterboro Airport as fast as you can. We'll get there in my new Cirrus. It can cruise at one hundred seventy knots and will get us there in three and a half hours. You can tell me more on the plane."

An hour later, the pilot of Carmine's plane announced that the passengers would have to deplane and take the next flight to Atlanta which left in another hour and thirty minutes. Carmine alerted Blake of his new scheduled arrival time and headed for the new departure gate. He was on the new plane in an hour, and soon took off for Atlanta.

Claire took her new Cirrus SR-22 to twelve thousand feet as Dreyfus explained, "I've given him several homing devices that he takes every time he expects to see Phil Blake. He swallows one and it sits in his belly so it's not detectable on the outside. The trouble is it only has a range of a few thousand meters and can't be detected by our tracker receiver unless we're in the same neighborhood. If I knew in advance that he was going to Atlanta, I would have made sure I was there to keep track of him. So now we've got to find him before Phil harms him."

"Here Harlan," Claire said, "Strap on this tube with the Velcro strap, so it stays in your nose. It will give you a steady flow of Oxygen which we'll need at seventeen thousand feet."

Claire's Oxygen tube was already in place. She adjusted the throttle to increase the airspeed. "This plane can go faster at seventeen thousand feet."

Carmine took a cab from the Atlanta Airport to Phil's headquarters in downtown Atlanta.

In Phil's seventeenth floor office, the thick, plush drapes hid the magnificent view of downtown Atlanta. Phil greeted Carmine almost warmly, but suggested that all electrical gadgets be put in a "safe place." He took his mobile phone and put it in the upper drawer of his desk and held out his hand to Carmine indicating that he wished to do the same with Carmine's.

"I know it's pretty stuffy and dark in this office," said Phil, "How about if we all take a small walk and talk things over in the sunlight? The sunlight and open air are good. It'll help to get a frank and open discussion."

The two men stepped out into the warm Georgia sunshine and headed down Piedmont Avenue, walking between the stone buildings of Georgia State University on their right and the towering Grady Memorial Hospital on their left.

Carmine was thinking of asking if Phil was still interested in joining the Network, when Phil asked him bluntly, "Are you still interested in becoming governor of New York State?"

Carmine hedged. "Maybe, but now's not the time. I'd rather not depend on help from Payne Strong. Don't want to owe him anything."

Phil stared at him. "No matter when y'all decide to run, you'll still owe **me** big time!"

Carmine was puzzled and stared at Phil.

"Want to know why you'll owe me, Mister Clean?" and without waiting for an answer, "Because nobody seems to know about you being a murderer, and if you don't go along with me and Strong, I'll end your political career PDQ! I know all about you and Bulova Johnny who one day, got shot in the back of the head by none other than Mr. Clean himself."

They turned left on Martin Luther King Jr. Drive. Carmine still didn't reply.

"Y'all don't believe me do ya? Well I got it from one of your buddies in Bensonhurst. Remember Bidetto Passalacqua? He was there at the time. Everybody there knew about it."

Claire consulted her map and looked for Hartzfield Airport, their destination in Atlanta. She called the airport for clearance to land. She lowered the plane's altitude reducing the distance to Carmine's radio transmitter and in preparation for landing.

Dreyfus scrutinized his tracker for signs of Carmine's radio frequency. He heard a single blip and an arrow on its screen pointed south, south west. "I think I've got him!" he shouted. Harlan had the Atlanta FBI office on his phone. He alerted them to Carmine's situation and continually updated them on Carmine's location.

Claire descended to two thousand feet.

"They're near the Cemetery!" Harlan shouted into the phone.

At Oakland Avenue Phil motioned to Carmine to follow him into Oakland Cemetery, one of Atlanta's most beautiful spaces. They walked silently through magnolia lined pathways and moved aside as a tour of six people on Segways passed them on their way to Martha Mitchell's gravesite.

Phil led Carmine out of Oakland Cemetery, across the street, to a fenced smaller, tree-lined cemetery and they continued their walk. This place was quieter than Oakland Cemetery and Carmine saw only one person besides Phil nearby. The man was about Carmine's height and weight, and was dressed like him.

Phil took another tack, "How's your daughter Claire and her boyfriend Milocchio?"

"Claire's fine but Iz is still missing. You wouldn't have any idea where he is, would you Phil?"

They came to an open gravesite. Carmine could see that it was deep, deeper than gravesites he recalled at the funerals he had attended.

"Y'all are asking **me** what happened to my friend Iz?" shouted Phil, over the noise of a nearby airplane. "Why don't you ask your daughter? The two of them were thick a while ago, thick enough for her to have gotten into his apartment and knocked him off!"

Carmine had had enough. Phil was not going to join the Network. And why were they standing next to a ten foot hole in the ground?

"Looks like we're not going to get to work together," snorted Phil. "The bitch must have got him! She must have found out that Milocchio hired Facciabrutta to kill you. She was the only one who could have got to him. He was my real choice to work with me and Strong and become Governor of New York. All we had to do was to get rid of you and have that Yale wimp become head of the Network. That would have been sweet! It'll be great to nail your daughter for Milocchio's murder. I'll find a way. That is, unless y'all change your mind in the next few minutes. Last chance Yankee!"

The other man in the background was advancing on them with a drawn nine millimeter Glock and Phil had removed what appeared to be a TASER, disguised as a large fountain pen from his pocket. Carmine's path was blocked by Phil and the other man was approaching. Carmine retreated in the only direction that was available, backwards towards the gaping hole.

Harlan shouted into the phone. "They're in the small cemetery right near the big one. They've got Carmine backed up against a hole in the ground. Looks like one of 'em has a weapon!"

Claire could see the men below and the hole behind Carmine. No time for an airport now. She lowered the nose of the Cirrus and aimed directly at them.

Phil continued, "See the deep hole? Deep enough for two. We're going to have a funeral tomorrow. We're going to bury a dear friend who knows too much. Of course, he's not dead yet, but he will be by tomorrow. Y'all won't mind sharing this hole with Passalacqua though. You'll be on the bottom, a few feet underneath. Usually when they dig up bodies, they stop at the first one they come to. So nobody's likely to find you for at least a few hundred years, when some anthropologist comes wandering by, thinking "Strange, these Twenty First Century Americans were, burying them two deep. They must also have been short of room. Why didn't they bury them vertically like we do?"

Phil advanced toward Carmine with the TASER in his hand, as the advancing plane descended rapidly in their direction. Carmine backed up towards the hole when the powerful gust of wind from the plane flying a few feet overhead blew Phil backwards away from Carmine but blew Carmine backwards towards the hole. Carmine tried to catch himself and hold onto the edge of the earth at the side of the hole. The earth gave way and Carmine plunged into the hole.

Chapter 66

Wayne watched the emergency medical technicians roll Carmine into the ER of Grady Memorial Hospital. Carmine lay on a stiff board on top of the stretcher. He wasn't moving. They were not doing CPR. Was that because he was OK or because he was dead? Wayne couldn't see if he was breathing.

Carmine opened his eyes. "I feel like I just rose from the dead," he muttered.

"Close," said one of the EMTs, "we did drag you out of your grave you know."

An FBI agent who had been at the scene stood by as the attendants gingerly moved Carmine from the stretcher onto a bed. Other agents had accompanied Phil Blake to a police precinct along with his accomplice. The accomplice not only resembled Carmine, he was wearing a similar hat and coat to Carmine's. Dreyfus later figured that Phil planned to return with Carmine's double and drive him to the airport. Of course, "Carmine" would never arrive back in New York City.

A nurse arrived and supervised the attendants' removal of Carmine's clothing. She put in an IV, and ordered a portable X ray. A technologist did an ECG.

Meanwhile, Carmine couldn't help overhearing the conversation in the next bed. A perturbed intern was interrogating the elderly wife of an even more elderly man. "This is an ER!"

said the intern, "Why did you bring him here for a blood pressure check? Why didn't you bring him to the clinic?"

"Well, it's hard to move him since his stroke. You know, he's partly paralyzed."

"Is he hemiplegic?"

"No, he's Irish." said the woman.

Carmine laughed gently. "Good," thought Dreyfus, who had just arrived with Claire, "he's waking up and must have been listening."

A doctor began interviewing Carmine. "So you were in a cemetery mindin' your own business, and an airplane came and blew you into a big grave? That right?"

Claire waited for the X ray reports and the assurance that Carmine had only a mild concussion and two broken ankles. Then she left Carmine's side and called Magda, to tell her what had happened.

When she returned, Carmine was fully awake. "Dreyfus," he asked, "What were those big capsules you sent me to swallow before I saw Phil each time?" Carmine inquired.

"They were mini GPS locating devices so we could find you in a hurry, just in case we lost track of you."

Chapter 67

Carmine was in his hospital room, his legs, with their freshly pinned ankles and new splints, were suspended by a rope and pulley, to just above the level of his heart.

Magda had arrived at his bedside moments before and had just finished alternately covering him with kisses and berating him for nearly getting killed.

Magda told him "Earlier today, Representative Enoch Carter called saying he traced some anonymous contributions to his Harlem College Scholarship Fund for needy students to you, Carmine. He said he thought of returning them to you but decided to thank you instead. Dr. Carter sends his good wishes for your speedy recovery and thanks for the contributions."

"I always hoped that he would come around." said Carmine. He's a good man. I value his support."

Claire sat in a chair nearby and both she and Magda were relieved when Carmine asked if they would mind very much if he reconsidered a career in politics? He decided that being a businessman and former gangster might be dangerous enough. Magda stood up quickly and said, "Got to pee," and dashed off to the toilet.

"She's been doing that a lot lately," thought Carmine.

Claire got up and sat in the chair next to his bed, and announced, "Glad you made it." And put her head on his shoulder.

Carmine looked at her lovingly. "Phil says you must have killed Iz. I suppose he'll be hard at work trying to prove you did it. Are you worried?"

"Not really," she said. "I'm glad you got me those hair pins and that Uncle Andy taught me how to use them. But all I had to do to clear myself was to answer three questions for Dreyfus while I was strapped to a polygraph machine."

"How'd you do?"

"The first question was, 'Did you kill Milocchio?'"

"I answered. 'I think so.'"

"Then they asked me, 'How did he die?'"

"I answered 'He must have died from a broken heart. After all, I broke up with him three months ago. It must have been a broken heart.'"

"The last question was, 'Other than you, is there anyone else you know of, who could have killed him?'"

"I answered, 'No,' and that was it. I'm no longer a suspect."

Epilogue

Facciabrutta survived his gunshot wound and bruised legs. He retired from his previous profession, and concentrated on card counting at black jack in casinos all over the globe. He is never recognized or remembered as a card counter. He is probably still at it. He also has figured out where the good slots are.

Durgayoni Ramalingam still lives in New York City, and cares for her son, who looks a lot like Devanta. She decided to remain single.

Devanta Singh finished his work on Krishnamycin at the Skirball Institute at N.Y.U. His brief marriage to Andjelkovic ended in divorce.

Andy Buonocore has recovered and is scheduled to be the grand capo of this year's Giglio.

Harlan Dreyfus became temporarily saddened when Claire decided that the two should become "just friends."

Wayne Wax had his ups and downs, but finally became a corporate attorney for Hadassah.

Magda got her PhD from Columbia. There was a reason for her urgency to pee. She also began having early morning nausea

Pepe Duvalliere enjoyed his two spouses and families. His wives are good friends. He chooses to believe they are unaware of each other.

Claire and Carmine: Maybe more of them later.

Network Members (Disciples)

Joseph **C**armine Cacciaguida, our protagonist.

Claire **Thomasina** Cacciaguida, his skeptical daughter, and manager of the Network.

Andrew Buonocore, Carmine's friend since childhood, and mob chief of Bensonhurst.

Nathaniel Barth, mob boss of lower Manhattan, except for Greenwich Village.

Jimmy Dadai Shi, (**"greatest"** in Mandarin), mob boss of eastern Long island.

Jaime Poquito, (**"small"** in Spanish,), immigrant from Puerto Rico, and mob boss of upper Manhattan and the Bronx.

John Evans, mob boss of Westchester County, (north of The Bronx.)

Thaddeus Gardner, mob boss of Newark, New Jersey.

J. (Judas) Isidoro Milocchio, ("a thousand eyes" in Italian,) and mob boss of Staten Island and lower Manhattan. Son of Rudolfo Malocchio, ("evil eye" in Italian).

Mila Matteiovna (**Mathew)** Grynzpan, a Russian Jewish immigrant and mob boss of Brighton Beach.

Pagianotis, (**Peter,** in Greek) Theophilus, mob boss of western Long Island.

Pepe, (**Phillip,)** Duvallier, a Haitian immigrant who controls the Flatbush area of Brooklyn.

Simon Tanner, mob boss of the borough of Queens.

BLISS

Gruen awoke as from a deep sleep, to find himself in the embrace of a large creature, her puckered lips pressed against his, her tongue struggling to enter his mouth, her soft amber colored hair covering his ears.

Ears! What ears? He had no ears. At least he had none until now. And what was this large creature on top of him, grinding her pelvis onto his, her gold crown bumping onto his crown with each pelvic thrust?

"Crown! What crown? Why crowns?"

He reached up to touch his crown and saw his hand. His hand! It was huge. It had five fingers, and one of them was a thumb, and the hand was a pale sad color and not bright and cheerful green as it always was before. He gently disentangled himself from the creature and tried to hop from the rock on which they lay, to the edge of his pond, to see himself reflected in the water.

"Hop" he thought, but hop, he couldn't. His now long legs were poorly formed for hopping. He stood up. His head was suddenly so high that he was frightened. His perspective of the world was always from just a few inches from ground level. Now he was way up in the air. He looked down at his image in the surface of the pond.

He was huge and pale and shaped like the creature who was now tugging at his pants leg.

Clothes! He had clothes! He was like the large animals that would sometimes come to the pond and skim stones on it. And his crown was loose and ready to fall off his head.

The creature tugged again.

She got off the rock and moved to his side, leading him in front of her on a path to her castle. She walked to his side and only slightly behind him and rubbed the soft protruding parts of the front of her upper body into the back of his arm. Her skin felt nice but rather dry, not wet and slippery like that of Gruenella, his female companion in the pond.

He waited outside the castle while the creature talked to her mother. The castle was rather small and run down.

"You did WHAT with a frog!" screamed her mother the Queen.

"PRINCE, what PRINCE?" she groaned, "Who are his mother and father? Prince of what? Where is his castle? Did you use protection? What will the neighbors say? What will YOUR FATHER say?"

A moment or two later a loud male voice demanded "What did that frog do to you Gwynneth?"

"He didn't do anything. The "Guidebook for Princesses" says just go to a pond and kiss a frog," she said, "and, if you're very lucky, the frog will turn into a prince. So that's what I did."

"What on earth were you thinking?" said the Queen. "Castles cost money to keep up! Times are tough. What kind of a match is a match with a FROG?"

"What about the blood lines?" moaned the King, "How will it look if our grandchildren are green and can only croak?"

His wife was quick with her answer to the king, "Don't tell me about blood lines. You're not so pure Anglo yourself! What about your ancestor Vikings who invaded a few hundred years ago?"

"Yeah, it was hardly worth the trouble. These people can't cook. Haven't had a good lutefisk in centuries."

"And what about your French ancestors who came later?"

At this, Gruen blanched as he could never have done before when he was green. He had heard from a pond snail about the treachery of the French and what they would do to small creatures like frogs and snails.

Gruen quietly withdrew from the castle and ran quickly to the edge of the pond. He saw Gruenella sunning herself on the large leaf of a water lily.

"Gruenella," he called to her, "It's me, Gruen." He remembered the quiet times he had known with her, and the moments of ecstasy when he mounted her and felt the clusters of eggs rub against his cloaca, when he spilled his semen over the eggs.

Gruenella, casually slid off the lily leaf and into the pond, unheeding. Gruen was now desperate. He threw off the crown and the clothes and dove into the water.

Gruenella slowly glided through the water just in front of him. Gruen struggled with all his might to catch her and was able to finally hold her gently in his larger human hand. He held her lips to his. At first she turned her head away, and then, after a few moments, she held them out to him for a gentle buss.

The two sat side by side again, their small green heads looking tenderly at each other just like old times.

She said, "It says in the "Girl Frog's Handbook", that if you kiss a prince and you're very lucky, he may turn into a great frog. So that's what I did."

So that's why, if you happen to be a prince, in the "Handbook for Princes," you will be warned to avoid ponds with girl frogs.

SPRING SCENT

Chapter 1

It was spring in New York City and the pretty red haired young woman smiled at the thirty four year old Victor Lebeau. She had never noticed him before as they often rode together on the train. They had never spoken. He hadn't the nerve and she had never made eye contact with him. Today, she smiled at him!

He enjoyed the moment, his 5 foot 6 inch, 145 pound frame swaying gently with the movement of the subway car, going from work in Manhattan to his apartment in Brooklyn. His grip was firm on the pole that supported him. Without warning, an older woman, who was sitting in front of him, offered him her seat. When he didn't accept it, she stood, gently pulled him from his hold on the pole, and pulled him into her seat. The car was crowded and a few nearby passengers turned to inspect the scene.

Victor was not accustomed to being noticed or to being the center of attention. He shrank into the unwanted seat. His shrinking, however, did not impede the woman from rubbing his knee with her thigh. Now Victor felt a strange combination of horror and fascination. As far back as he could remember, no girl or woman had ever made a pass at him. He tried moving his knee but the thigh followed. So Victor stopped trying and left his knee to the tender mercies of the thigh, which felt rather pleasant.

As he was adjusting to the warmth of the thigh, the woman grasped his arm and with a jerk, raised him upright and pulled him toward the door of the car. He was surprised at the strength of the woman who was determined and outweighed him by at least twenty five pounds.

Victor no longer protested as the woman led him by the arm up three flights of stairs to her tenement apartment. Without ceremony, she pulled him into her bedroom and towards her, pressing him against her pudgy body, her mouth pressed against his. Neither of them spoke. Victor began to tremble. He tentatively pushed his hand between them and touched her breast. She pulled him even closer to her and pressed herself against him. Still pressed together, they made their way to the bed and tumbled onto it. The woman hastily removed her clothing and tossed it onto the carpet, just to the side of the bed. Victor pulled off his shoes, pants, and shirt but in his underwear, he suddenly froze. His member was limp, just when he most needed it to cooperate.

They were now lying side by side on the bed. The woman caressed his limp member against her and it responded. Victor's anxiety subsided. It took only a few moments for them to have sex and reach climax and Victor was elated! Victor was thrilled! This was his first sex with another person, a real woman.

She lay facing him on the bed. She had a round, ruddy, quiet face. He noticed the mole on one side of her nose. There were bags under her eyes and wrinkles on her forehead. Her hair was dark brown with a hint of red, except for the roots that were gray.

Her cheeks ended in prominent jowls that hung from the sides of her face.

"My name is Amy." She said, "I'm 56 years old and this is the first time I did it since Harold, my husband, died eight years ago. Thank you."

"Me too, it was my first time" he said, and added "ever."

"He was a fireman, a good man, a good husband." She said, "See the picture over there on the wall? My two kids. He gave me two kids, and one miscarriage. They're all growed up now. He was a good husband." Suddenly shy, she pulled the bed sheet over herself. "I hope he wouldn't care that I did it. I can't believe I did it with you."

Victor said, "Whatever Harold would have thought, I think you're wonderful."

Now remorseful, and ignoring Victor's admiration, Amy continued, "A fireman. He died when a big construction crane fell over onto a building on fifty six[th] and Lexington, and I pull some stranger off the train and have sex with him. What kind of woman does that make me? But something about him made me do it. As soon as he got on the train, I knew it." And to Victor, "As soon as you came near me, I knew it. I wanted you. Why did you make me do it?"

Victor wondered at her sudden turn of emotions and began to dress, ready to make a hasty exit. "I made you do it? I was minding my own business before you pulled me off the train and brought me up here."

"You made me do it!" she yelled at him as he hurried out the door.

Chapter 2

The next morning, in his apartment, Victor brushed his teeth, shaved, and showered. He was careful to wash every inch that he could reach of his body, and was especially careful to wash his face thoroughly. It'd been a few years since his acne had acted up but he was still careful to wash it thoroughly. He applied his new after shave lotion, and deodorant, and dressed.

He hopped onto the subway car and all was as usual. Nobody noticed him. No one smiled at him or otherwise acknowledged his existence.

He exited the subway and walked the few remaining blocks to the Empire State Medical Center Hospital. Victor was a bacteriologist and directed the Microbiology Laboratory of the hospital. On the way to the clinical labs, he stopped at his research lab in the basement of the building. The sign next to his lab read Victor Lebeau, PhD. A hand written paper sign on the door, read "Meth Lab," his personal name for his lab which dealt with various types of methanogens, bacteria-like organisms that produce and are the main global sources of the gas methane. It was a one room lab with special equipment to grow and study these organisms which can only survive in an atmosphere without any oxygen. He put on his white lab coat and walked to the anaerobic chamber where the organisms were kept. He could move the contents of the chamber and examine them by inserting his hands into the two large rubber gloves that extended into it. The bases of the gloves were fixed to the front of the apparatus in an airtight manner. Victor pushed his hands into the gloves, and picked up and looked over each of the thin circular six inch diameter Petri dishes in the chamber. Each of these contained a layer of culture medium specially prepared for the growth of these fastidious organisms which grew in small discrete colonies on the surface of the media. The Petri dishes had loose covers that were easily removed to allow for working with the colonies. Other colonies were growing in the chamber in sealed small bottles containing similar culture material.

His research grant from the United States Department of Energy paid for him to examine new strains of methanogens. The cultures of these organisms arrived in vials labeled only with a number and were accompanied by a list of requirements needed for their growth. The list specified for each organism, the optimum temperature, composition of the gas within the chamber, and the nutrients needed in the culture medium. Victor's job was to measure the rate of methane production and then to do a DNA analysis of the single chromosome in these organisms and in the smaller amount of plasmid DNA outside the chromosome. The government was developing a database to find the genes that were associated with the highest methane production and with ease of growth in culture. The latest strain of organisms had arrived last week and this was the one now growing in the chamber.

Victor left the "Meth" Lab, ran up the two flights of stairs and entered the clinical lab complex. He moved past the Toxicology lab and noticed Polly working on her GCMS, an acronym for Gas Chromatography Mass Spectrometer. This was the lab's best machine to identify small amounts of substances of interest, like drugs, toxins, and products made by bacteria.

Polly was thin, five feet, two inches tall, with unadorned blonde hair and a thin long face without makeup. She wore a white lab coat over a wool sweater. Victor had a secret crush on Polly ever since she arrived two years ago. She was considerate and always said "Hello," when they met. She was the only woman who seemed to notice him but they rarely spoke to each other. Victor was sure that she would not accept so he had never asked her out.

Victor entered the Microbiology lab, donned another white lab coat, and examined the pile of requisitions and specimens that would determine this morning's work.

The first requisition accompanied a blood specimen from a twelve year old girl who had arrived four days ago from Bolivia with her newly immigrant parents. The clinical information on the requisition indicated that a week ago, she had developed fever and swelling of her left eyelids, redness of the eye, and swelling of the lymph nodes of the left side of her neck.

Victor pulled the cap off the tube and put a drop of blood from the tube onto each of two glass slides. He put the edge of a third slide into the drops of blood on the first two slides and smeared the blood across the surfaces of he slides forming a thin layer of blood on each of these two slides. He put one slide into a staining machine. Quickly, Victor put the other slide with the still wet blood, on the stage of his microscope. He used the high power objective, and looked at the blood. As he focused up and down and moved the slide across the stage, his attention was suddenly riveted to a tiny writhing microscopic creature on the slide.

He removed the other slide from the staining machine and put it onto the stage of his microscope. He moved the slide across the stage several times and finally spotted a stained example of the parasite he saw wriggling on the first slide. Now he could see its thin wavy form, its dark nucleus, and a flagellum, a thin whip-like structure that moved the parasite. He continued looking for another example and found one. In this one, at the base of the flagellum, there was a small dark round structure, a kinetoplast, which identified it as a type of protozoon parasite called a trypanosome. In Africa, species of this group of parasites cause sleeping sickness. In the Americas, another similar species causes Chaga's disease, (American Trypanosomiasis).

He checked his reference textbook and found that the child's symptoms fit with Chaga's disease but that there is also another similar appearing trypanosome which may be found in the blood but does not cause disease.

He called Doctor Pang, the physician who had ordered the blood smear test, and he recommended that she order other blood tests to look for antibodies that could distinguish between the harmless and the pathogenic trypanosomes.

"Thanks." said Dr. Pang, "We don't see much Chaga's Disease around here. If she has it, we'll be able to treat her early, before these little bugs invade her heart and cause heart failure. Would you mind if I came down to the lab in a little while to look at these Trypanosomes?"

Chapter 3

Victor usually had lunch at eleven thirty AM, when the lab staff's dining area was mostly empty. He would eat his ham and cheese sandwich and then an apple, and read from whatever was handy so that he could avoid eye contact with whoever happened to walk in. Most of the staff lunched at noon and he would often see Polly there with them, eating her sandwich and reading.

Today was going to be different. Maybe it was that he needed to share his triumphal diagnosis with someone or maybe it was last night's adventure, but he was going to talk to Polly today! She was seated alone at a table for two. Great!

"Would you mind very much if I sit at this table?" he asked, his palms sweaty and his heart pounding. He was suddenly embarrassed at the sight of his dorky brown paper bag lunch. Surprisingly, Polly smiled and said "No, please join me." He noticed her similar brown paper bag and sat down, reassured, across from her.

"How's your day going?" She asked.

"So, far, it's one of the best days I've had," he said, and added, "and it's getting better every minute." He felt his face flush. He was embarrassed and yet delighted that he had come up with something pleasant and clever for her.

Polly was pleased that he had finally shown some interest in her. She had seen him looking at her from a distance before, and she hoped he liked her. She was reticent to acknowledge his last comment as a compliment meant for her. Instead, she focused on his first response. "What's going on to make it such a good day for you?"

"I found a really exotic parasite on a blood smear of a twelve year old South American child, a parasite I had never seen before, and I think I may have helped save her life!"

"That's pretty exciting," she said, "and enough to make anyone's day. I'm glad for you."

"And it's getting better because I'm sitting here having lunch with you," an emboldened Victor replied.

They arranged to meet for lunch that Saturday.

Chapter 4

At four thirty in the afternoon, Victor was finishing up his work when Dr. Karen Pang danced in. She was a short, pretty, young Asian woman with large dark eyes and shiny black hair arranged in a ballet bun. Victor expected her to pirouette any moment but she settled in behind him, and smiled. "Where are the bugs you promised to show me?"

"I can't show you the living ones." he replied, "They're all dried up on the slide but I can show you the ones on the stained slide." He placed the slide on the stage and moved it until he found a trypanosome, moved his head out of the way, and motioned for Dr. Pang to look through the microscope over his shoulder. "It's right in the middle of the field, Dr. Pang. It's the wavy little protozoon with a flagellum."

"Please call me Karen," she said as she leaned over and peered through the scope. "Cute little bug isn't it!" She took a deep breath and seemed to continue looking through the scope, but Victor could smell her perfume and felt the distinct soft touch of her breast against his shoulder as she leaned over him.

She turned to him "You're cute too," she said as she gently rubbed the center of his back with her left hand. The right hand was still focusing the microscope. Then, she paused, abandoned the microscope, and said, "Come with me. I've got something for you." She gently tugged on his arm and motioned for him to follow her. A few moments later, she unlocked a door to a dark room in the hospital basement. "It's great to be an MD here. My passkey unlocks most rooms."

She did not turn on the light but Victor could make out the forms of instruments in what must be a storage facility for old and obsolete surgical instruments. He guessed that the hospital management could not bear to discard all of this expensive equipment so it sat, awaiting a useful future that never came.

Victor sensed that this adventure was going to be interesting but before he could reflect any longer, Karen was pressed firmly against him, her lips on his, her hands deftly undoing his clothing. Victor, in his mind now an experienced lover, was quick to follow suit. Their lovemaking was ardent and he was now certain that Karen was a dancer. She was graceful and, although there was no place to lie down in the cramped room, seemed to be able to bend her body into positions worthy of inclusion in the Kama Sutra, which he had studied from time to time in anticipation of an opportunity like this one. His joy was intense but short lived. As soon as they finished, Karen hurriedly dressed, mumbled a few words about being late to meet her husband, kissed him gently on the forehead, and rushed out of the room. "*Wait a minute,*" he thought, "*isn't it the woman who's supposed to want cuddling after sex?*"

On the way home from work that evening, the pretty woman with the red hair smiled at him and this time, said "Hi". He nodded to her. He scanned the subway car and was grateful that Amy was nowhere to be seen.

Chapter 5

It was Saturday, and as he dreaded, his Aunt Trudy was on the phone, "Victor, the radio says it's going to rain today. I know you threw out the galoshes I sent you, but please wear your rubbers so you don't get your feet wet and catch a cold!"

His uncle Bert mumbled loud enough for Victor to hear. "The only rubbers for him should be on his dick. He should go out and get laid." Victor was tempted to tell Uncle Bert about his good luck lately but if Aunt Trudy had worries about going out in the street without galoshes, she would panic at his current doings. He thought better of it and decided not to say anything.

As they had agreed, Victor met Polly at Mama Leone's restaurant in Manhattan. He had bought a new sport coat for the occasion. Polly had her hair cut and styled. It no longer hung from her head like a mop. She wore lipstick and eye liner and she had on a stylish black dress and red jacket. With the help of some critically positioned facial tissues, there was a suggestion of breasts under the dress. Her eyeglasses were hidden away in her purse, in case she might really need them.

Victor was pleased and more at ease than he had ever before been in the company of a woman.

Polly was elated with her first date in over a year. The last one had been with a Russian waiter who was alarmed that she had no hair on her legs or armpits.

"Where is de hair?" he had asked, staring at her legs. "I have hair where it counts!" she had exclaimed, not knowing exactly what she meant and not intending to let him find out.

Back in the present, seated across the table from her, Victor said, "You look beautiful," and then added "That's a good start."

"Start of what?" she teased. Polly loved his new sport coat, and was happy to see Victor so confident and relaxed. She had waited months for him to ask her out and now hoped she wouldn't scare him off. She looked away from his startled gaze and pretended to look at the menu.

He picked up his own menu and, his confidence a bit shaken, wondered about a proper answer to her question. "A good start to a perfect evening." He finally replied, and ordered a bottle of Chianti. He needed to be careful. Polly actually listened to what he said and answered him. The last two women he had encountered talked to themselves, only pausing to allow him to say something that they didn't appear to hear. Although he couldn't exactly say that Polly took what he said seriously, with her it was definitely a two-way conversation.

In order to examine her lipstick, which she feared has smeared onto her lip, Polly removed a small mirror from her purse, held it in front of her but beneath the level of the table top, out, she hoped, of Victor's view. Without her glasses, she saw only a blur. She tried to feel the suspect area of lip. At that moment, she saw Victor staring quizzically at her. She quickly removed her finger from her mouth, and accidentally brushed it by her cheek, leaving the cheek with a small red smear. Quickly, covering, she asked, "Victor, you were telling me about a parasite that you found in a child. Tell me more about it please."

Victor smiled. This was his strong suit. "It was Chaga's disease, and it's caused by a one celled parasite called Trypanosoma cruzii."

Surreptitiously, putting the mirror back in her purse, Polly asked, "How did she get it?"

Victor, wondered what Polly was doing behind the table top but answered, "The parasite is carried by small mammals and spread by bugs called kissing bugs or assassin bugs. The bugs live in houses in cracks in the walls and sneak out at night and bite people. When they bite, they also leave droppings with the parasite eggs on the skin. The bitten area itches and when the person scratches, he pushes the parasite eggs into the wound, or sometimes, rubs his eyes and spreads the parasite to the membranes of the eye. That's what happened to this little girl. She must have rubbed her eyes and she had swelling around the eye and fever, when the Trypanosome spread into her blood."

"And you found it in her blood?"

"Yes," said Victor, with an attempt at modesty, "They're not really difficult to identify."

The waiter returned and they ordered their meals. Polly had rehearsed some other conversation starters and she asked, "I see you almost every day but I hardly know you at all. What would you like to tell me about yourself?"

Victor hesitated. *"What can I tell her that won't bore her to tears?"* he thought, but said. "My father is French. He was a war correspondent for Le Figaro. My mother was Jewish. She was a nurse and was a civilian working for the U.S Army in Vietnam when they met." And then, to spice things up, he quoted from Danny Kaye's song, *Anatole of Paris,* from a film he made in 1947, "And I'm the result of this twisted eugenics, of this family of inbred schizophrenics, the end of a long, long line of bats! I design (pause) women's hats."

To his amazement, she nonchalantly continued the song, "You're Anatole of Paris, you cannot vex, the daffy sex. They want shrubs from the prairie, grubs from the dairy, they learn to wear the stern of the Queen Mary."

And Victor took over, "And why do I sew each new chapeau with a style they will look positively grim in?"

And Polly finished with, "Strictly between us, entre nous, you hate women."

Victor was surprised and delighted. He didn't seem to mind that several sets of eyes from adjacent tables were looking at them curiously. "Where did you learn that song? It's not what you hear on the radio every day or even every decade."

"Polly was equally delighted to have made a hit with Victor. "My mother was a big Danny Kaye fan. She used to rent his films. I must have seen *Hans Christian Andersen*, and *The Secret Life of Walter Mitty* a half dozen times. She had an album of his records, seventy eights. I finally got rid of them when my mother's old Victrola phonograph broke and we couldn't play seventy eights any more." And then in mock seriousness, she asked, "So do you really hate women?"

Victor was again startled by Polly's ability to bring him up sharply but was beginning to enjoy the challenge. "I'm afraid I don't have enough experience with women to have formed an opinion about all of them. But I know one woman that I definitely don't hate. In fact, I like her a lot."

Chapter 6

The new Victor decided to take himself more seriously. Now that he seemed able to attract women, why shouldn't he look more the part? It would be good to add some muscle to his puny frame. He joined the YMCA and took an evening aerobic workout class.

The class leader was a muscular woman named Olga, with a shaved head except for a small clump of short hair that was neatly allowed to grow over her left ear. She was dressed in Spandex clothing and glistened as she moved onto and off of a step stool, swinging her arms and barking out instructions to the participants who mimicked what she did. Victor was inept and seemed to be the only one in the class who had not already had similar classes. Olga noted his difficulty and began to pay him special attention, slowing down the exercise to allow him time to catch up to the class. After a while, she moved to a step stool directly in front of Victor who had just about given up. She stayed nearby until the session was over.

As the class broke up, Olga approached him and instructed him to follow her. She expected to be obeyed. She led him into a room marked "Employees Only," and in a moment, had him in a viselike grip.

"Here we go again," thought Victor but he hadn't the inclination, and certainly not the strength to stop her. *"I might just as well relax,"* he thought as her hairy groin was pushed against his mouth. Olga was not much inclined to deep conversation but admitted afterwards, "You are my first man in a long time."

Victor was beginning to tire of his sudden attractiveness to strong women who push him around even if he liked what they did.

"*I think I'll switch to the strength training room with the weights,*" he thought.

But, most interesting to Victor, was the question. "What's happened all of a sudden to these women?" or even more intriguing, "What could have happened to me that attracted them?"

Chapter 7

A week had gone by and Victor sorted through his clinical cases for the new day. This morning he was sleepy and hung over. The woman from apartment Three B came over last night. They had met earlier that evening at the mailboxes at the entrance to his apartment building. It was ten PM when she appeared at his door with a measuring cup and asked if she could borrow "a cup of sex." She had, in her other hand, a bottle of cheap red wine that she insisted he share with her. The result was that this morning, he had a headache, a sour stomach, and a problem staying awake.

Most of his cases for this day were stool specimens sent for evaluation for parasites. In the pile there was also a urine specimen from a young man who has just returned an assignment as Peace Corp volunteer in the small nation of Burkina Fasso. He noted on his return to the USA, that his urine was bloody and that it hurt to urinate.

Victor put the urine into a conical tube and spun it in a centrifuge, spilled off the liquid, and was left with a little button of sediment at the bottom. He examined the sediment with his microscope and was not surprised to see among the red blood cells and mucus, a number of parasite eggs with tan clear walls, and a tiny wriggling wormlike creature within each one. The walls of a few ova were open and a few of the small creatures that had hatched from the eggs could be seen swimming among the rest of the sediment. Victor saw a small spine at the ends of each ovum and knew that they were the eggs of parasitic worms that lived in the veins of this young man's bladder. The parasite was named Schistosoma hematobium.

He noticed a medical student walking past his lab bench. The student, recognizable as such by her youth and her short white medical student's coat, was taking a month of her senior year of medical school, studying in the lab. Among Victor's many self-recognized faults, was a proclivity to show off his diagnostic prowess under the guise of teaching students. "Hey, there!" he shouted, "Come over here and look at this parasite." The puzzled student, turned toward Victor, "You mean me?" she said.

"Of course I mean you," he replied.

"My name is on my ID badge," she said, pointing to it. It was a long South Asian name, not clearly visible to Victor.

"Sorry," he said, and pointing to the stage of his microscope, he asked "What's this? Hint- It's a spun down urine sediment from a young man just back from Africa who waded in streams all day."

"Were there snails in the streams?" she asked, letting him know that she knew the answer." The life cycle of these worms, they both knew, involved certain species of snails. The little creatures that hatched from the eggs would reach ponds and streams, and would infect and develop inside the snails. The snails would release the next phase of the parasite, one that would enter the skin of a person who was wading in the pond or stream and then move to the urinary tract of that person. There they would develop into adult worms that would be shed eggs into the urine to complete the cycle.

Victor was surprised and pleased that she knew the identity of the parasite. "Could he have gotten this disease here in New York?' he asked. "No," she said, there are no snails here that can be intermediary hosts to these Schistosomes."

"A plus! that's your new name." said Victor, thoroughly impressed, as she and her dark eyes and long black hair turned from him and walked away.

She turned back to him momentarily and replied "Milind is your new name. In my native language, it means "bee that flits from flower to flower."" Then she was gone.

"What did she mean by that?" he thought. It was now nine thirty in the morning. His hangover was gone. He was suddenly surprised that this student was not interested in him. He had gone, in a few weeks, from never expecting any regard from women to a state where he was surprised if he received none. *"Victor, back to reality,"* he mused. *"You're still a nerd after all, and what's with this "bee" business?"*

At noon, he had lunch with Polly and they arranged to see each other every Saturday for dinner and a movie or a show. Having lunch with Polly had quickly become the highlight of each day. They could talk, really talk, and she was concerned about what he was thinking, how he felt, and happy that he was now more outgoing. Victor's one problem was that he couldn't tell her about his recently developing exhilarating but exhausting night life. He also wondered why Polly wasn't affected by his recent sexual magnetism that seemed to overcome other women. He pondered in between examining the stool specimens about the possible cause of his sudden sexual prowess. He thought of his new aftershave lotion. He found this new lotion packaged with a similar deodorant stick on the lowest shelf in the CVS pharmacy that he frequented. The more expensive, highly advertised products were on the upper shelves. The label on the package was a simple black and white Yin/Yang symbol and the word "It" The two were packaged together in plastic wrap and were on sale together for ninety-nine cents. Victor couldn't resist a bargain. He bought one of the three packages on the shelf. The fragrances of the lotion and the deodorant were mild, but pleasant, and smelled vaguely of cinnamon. The lotion and deodorant were likely suspects because he had used them for only a few days before his subway abduction and introduction to the pleasures of his newly found but not always welcome seductive powers.

The problem with the aftershave lotion being the cause was that women didn't seem to notice him in the morning when the scent of the lotion was strongest. The medical student hardly seemed aware of him. All of his adventures had occurred in the late afternoon and evening when there seemed to be no remaining cinnamon scent." *There must be,*" he thought, "*some other cause.*"

Chapter 8

Several weeks had now passed since the dramatic change in Victor's life and he had settled into a pattern of having lunch with Polly on weekdays, spending his Saturdays with her, and having brief encounters with other women in the evenings. More often though, Victor would try to shrink into his surroundings and avoid public places in the evenings. The excitement of these adventures was beginning to wane.

Saturday came and he took Polly to a concert performance of Rogers and Hammerstein songs at Carnegie Hall. Somehow, Victor related more to the romantic songs from the 1950s and earlier, than to current more sophisticated and worldly songs. "Schmaltz," Polly called his taste in music, but she seemed to enjoy these as much as he did. Polly's head nestled softly on his shoulder as Billy Bigelow and Julie Jordan looked tenderly at each other and sang, "If I loved you, words wouldn't come in an easy way." Victor's arm curled around her shoulders as they sang "longing to tell you but afraid and shy, I'd let my golden chances pass me by."

Polly held a handkerchief to her nose. Victor was moved. *"She's crying,"* he thought, but Polly always kept the handkerchief close at hand in the spring when the pollen count was high and her nose would become stuffed and might run at any time. Maybe it was the pollen count and maybe it was the love song. Not even Polly knew for sure, but she hoped Victor would not let too many golden chances pass him by. She had thought that his apparent lack of interest in sex with her was due to his obvious shyness and inexperience but she wondered if there could not be another reason. On the other hand, he seemed very interested in her and seemed to enjoy her company. She wasn't about to let this relationship remain platonic. She was determined to kiss him that night.

After dinner, he walked with her to her apartment, and responded nicely, she thought to her kiss. Victor was surprised by the kiss and found that he enjoyed its tenderness more than the hurried, ruffled sex that he had been having lately with the seemingly faceless and somehow anonymous women who had pursued him. Victor accepted Polly's offer of a cup of coffee in her apartment. They sat across from each other at the kitchen table.

"You told me that your mother was a Jewish nurse who met your father in Viet Nam. What was she like?" asked Polly.

"I can't really say since she died from a complication of childbirth soon after I was born."

"That must have been tough for you and tough for your father. If he was a war correspondent, who took care of you after your mother died?

"My father had three sisters who lived in France. I lived with them and they rotated me from one to another for my first five years. After that, they all got tired of having me around so I stayed with a good friend of my mother in Brooklyn. I call her "Aunt" Trudy. She was in her late thirties and single at the time and I guess I was the closest thing to a child of her own that she could imagine in her future. She got married fifteen years ago which was about when I went away to school, much to the relief of my new "Uncle" Bert."

"What about your father? Do you ever see him?"

"Not since I lived with Trudy. She and my father never got along. So I haven't seen him in many years and I didn't see much of him before that either."

"*How sad,*" thought Polly.
Victor left right after the coffee.

Chapter 9

That Monday morning, Victor entered his "Meth Lab", donned his lab coat, and sat down in front of the anaerobic chamber. The chamber was constructed of flexible polyvinyl. Materials were introduced and removed through an airlock located on the side. The gas in the chamber contained small amounts of Carbon Dioxide and Hydrogen which were the building blocks used by the methanogens to make methane. The remainder of the gas was Nitrogen. All traces of Oxygen had to be kept out of the chamber because methanogens are unable to survive in its presence. In fact, since small amounts of Oxygen can enter the chamber every time the airlock is opened, and some Oxygen diffuses through the plastic housing of the chamber, the chamber also contains an apparatus to remove any stray Oxygen that enters.

Victor put his hands into the gloves which extended into the chamber and arranged the glass culture bottles on a circular moving platform that rotated. Above the assembly line was a probe that was robotically inserted one after another, into the circular membranes on the tops of each of the bottles to measure the methane concentration in the bottles.

Methanogens belong to the group of microorganisms called Archaea, primitive bacteria-like organisms which are most common at great depths near the bottoms of oceans or ponds, in decaying organic matter, and in the intestinal tracts of herbivores and other creatures where there is little or no Oxygen. "*Strange,*" he thought, "*that organisms can adapt to almost any hostile environment on the planet. Some of the Archaea live in hot springs hot enough to burn human skin.*"

Then he wondered if the methanogens could in some way be related to his sudden attractiveness. "*Could they be growing on his skin? Could they produce pheromones that were attractive to women?*" He had long ago learned that pheromones provided a means of chemical attraction in many species of animals, large and small. It was questionable if they were important in humans although there was some strong evidence that they were.

He took a new sterile Petri dish, scraped the skin of his face on a sterile wooden tongue blade, smeared the stick over the surface of the enriched agar medium on the Petri dish, and put it into the anaerobic chamber through the airlock. "*Did methanogens,*" he wondered, "*somehow get from the cultures in the Petri dishes onto his skin?*" He would know if they grew in the anaerobic chamber. It would probably take two weeks to know if these slow growing creatures were not present. But if they were present, some might show up sooner.

The next Friday morning, as Victor lay in bed at 5 AM, he again wondered about a possible role of the aftershave lotion. Could it be that the change in him was only indirectly related to it?

He got an idea and sought out Polly as soon as he got to work.

"Polly," he excitedly asked, "Could you do me a favor, a professional favor, a big favor?"

Polly listened intently and agreed to do what he asked. Later that afternoon she took a piece of tissue that Victor had rubbed on the surface of his face, and she began an extraction of the oily substance from the paper. The extraction would be ready by Monday.

Chapter 10

On Saturday afternoon Polly was primping for her date with Victor that evening. They would be going to Chez Josephine, a pleasant but elegant French restaurant in the theater district of Manhattan where they played music recorded in the 1930s by Josephine Baker, for whom the restaurant was named. Polly knew that Victor was a fan. Nineteen thirties, that was about right for Victor's taste. He was definitely stuck in the first half of the twentieth century. She thought about how happy she was to be working with Victor on this new project. He was excited but secretive about it. She was hoping that he would share more of the details with her in time and that they would become even closer because of it. It was good that the restaurant was in Manhattan not far from Victor's apartment. Maybe he would be more relaxed and romantic at his apartment than when they were at hers.

After dinner, she invited herself to his place and she was surprised that Victor was very willing to take her there. They had shared an expensive bottle of delicious Gevrey Chambertin that she offered to buy, and Victor was enjoying the slightly woozy after effects. "Good," she thought, "I got him drunk. He's mine tonight!"

They climbed the stairs to his fifth floor walk up apartment. It was modestly furnished except for a Nineteenth Century era large ornate wall clock with a marble face with roman numerals indicating the hours, and the words "Manfredi" and "Charleville" painted on it to indicate the maker and the city in which it was made. The wooden case contained the mechanism and the small pendulum that hung from it. The oval wooden front of the case was inlaid with clusters of mother of pearl.

"It's an "oeil de boeuf," (bull's eye) clock. Remarkable, isn't it?" asked Victor.

Polly looked at this anachronistic piece and sighed, "It's beautiful. How did you get it?"

"It was a gift from my three French aunts when I left for the States to live with Aunt Trudy. I think they had it somewhere in an attic. I don't remember seeing it there. I don't remember very much from my time with them in France. I can't even speak French. But I love that clock. I kept it in my room at Trudy's place and at the apartments I've had since then. I think it's been like a security blanket for me. Wherever it is, is home to me."

"*This poor soul definitely needs someone to care about him*," she thought, but said, "Do you have trouble being close to someone else?"

"I don't think so. I just haven't found anyone who wants to be close with me."

Polly was touched and wanted desperately to hold him and love him. She wanted to be wanted as much as he did. She gently pulled him to the sofa, caressed his face, and kissed him on the sides of his neck and then full on the lips. They both had tears in their eyes as they embraced. Polly stood and motioned Victor to the bedroom. Victor put one hand under her knees, the other hand under her back, carried her into the bedroom and placed her gently on the bed.

They each took turns removing one piece of clothing from the other until they were both nude. It was spring but it was cold enough that they withdrew under the covers and continued exploring each other, with their hands and with their mouths. Polly caressed him and quietly whispered, "Where do you keep the condoms?"

"In the upper drawer of the night stand." He whispered back.

Polly reached over to the nightstand, felt a drawer handle, and without looking at it, pulled it open. She reached in and felt soft, silky pieces of clothing. She bolted upright, and stared into the drawer. It was the lower drawer and it was stuffed with silk panties and brassieres in various sizes and colors, a few scattered other pieces of women's apparel, two tubes of lipstick, and a box of tampons.

Chapter 11

Polly hadn't shown up at work on Monday. Tuesday morning, as Victor entered the lab, she was facing her GCMS machine and did not turn to look at him. He could see that her eyes were red and she looked as if she had been crying. She did not return his greeting. She had not answered her phone or returned his voicemail messages since her abrupt departure from his apartment. How could he possibly explain to her that he had simply put in that drawer all of the articles left behind in his apartment by women who had hurriedly left right after having sex with him? If they ever came back he could return them. He couldn't explain anything to her anyway since she wouldn't talk to him.

So he called the only other person he could talk with. "Aunt Trudy," he was holding back tears, "I'm miserable."

Aunt Trudy was hard of hearing and always had her speaker phone on so she could hear better. Uncle Bert's voice announced, "He finally figured out that he's miserable. Tell him he needs to get laid."

"That's the trouble," Victor said. "My girl friend found all the panties and bras in my drawer."

"You have a girl friend?" asked Trudy, and to Bert, "He has a girl friend!" and to Victor, Is she Jewish?"

"Why should she be Jewish? I'm not Jewish." moaned Victor.

"Your mother was Jewish, so to Jews and anti semites, you're Jewish."

"Right now, I'm miserable enough without being Jewish."

"You even sound Jewish when you complain, like now. And how can you have a girl friend without telling me about it? How could you do that to me?"

And from Bert, "What's with the bras and the panties, Victor?"

Victor hung up the phone.

On Wednesday morning he was doing his methane analyses when he got the sense that someone was watching him. There was a small window in the door of the lab and a woman's face moved away from the window as he turned to look at it. It was not a face he recognized.

Up in the clinical labs, he noticed a woman who walked through his area, briefly glanced at him, and left saying nothing. In the cafeteria, as he sat alone eating his lunch, he thought that some women at a nearby table were glancing in his direction, and smiling among themselves. He thought he heard one of the women say. "He's not so hot!"

Chapter 12

Another week went by and the culture from the skin of his face did not grow any methanogens. So, the methanogens couldn't be the source of his peculiar attractiveness, and his current troubles. Then he got an email from Polly, "Come over this evening. Bring flowers." He arrived with a dozen red roses and rang the doorbell. She let him in and seemed calm. "I've been thinking a lot about us and I know what you were doing. It's really unfair of me to be angry with you about it."

Victor sighed with relief and joy. "I didn't think you would be so understanding." he said. "I never meant to hurt you and I promise I won't do it anymore."

"Victor, you need to be who you are and I'm ready to live with you the way you are," and whispering, "as long as you don't do it in public."

"I never did it in public."

"There are lots of worse habits and I don't see how your putting on a bra and panties in your apartment once in a while is going to be a problem. So, I'm sorry about getting so upset with you. It was my fault. I hope you'll forgive me."

Victor was silent for a moment. *"She thinks I sneak around the house wearing bras and panties,"* he thought. *"She doesn't know about the other women."*

Part of Victor was disappointed that she believed he was a cross dresser and that part wanted to shout out that he was a stud but the sane part of him decided to go along with this lucky break. "I've already thrown out all of that stuff from the drawer and I'm finished with them forever. I promise never to do anything to hurt you again." And he meant it.

Polly looked thoughtfully at him and asked, "Are you curious about what I found in the sample from your face? I've been working on it with the GCMS like you asked me to, and there is one substance in it that looks like it's related to or is a 16-androstene, a metabolite of testosterone. These are volatile products secreted by the apocrine sweat glands of the armpit, the groin, and to a lesser extent on the face. There's only a very little bit of it in the sample but it's unusual. I haven't quite nailed it down yet but I think it's androstenol. I'll keep you posted on what develops. I really want to know what you're looking for and I'm not sure I'll tell you what it is if you don't tell me what's going on."

Chapter 13

The next morning Victor took a sample of sweat from his armpit with a sterile Q-tip and sent it to Polly. The phone rang and he answered it. Few people knew the number to his lab and he received very few calls on that line.

"I'm Joe Birnbaum from the Brooklyn Raptor and I want to of do a piece on scientists who work at the University Hospital. Interesting stuff, like discovering unusual diseases. I hear you found some pretty rare parasites recently. Would you have a few minutes to talk with me about what you do and maybe show me around your lab? I think this topic would make very interesting copy for our readers. They like unusual medical cases. And it would be good press for your hospital and the University," said the pleasant voice at the other end of Victor's phone line.

The Raptor was a weekly tabloid newspaper which concentrated on scandals and exposes, especially focusing on celebrities and politicians. Victor was pleased that they would be doing something constructive, publicizing science and medicine.

Victor greeted Joe at the hospital entrance and escorted him to the clinical labs. Joe seemed interested in the parasites that Victor showed him but he was more interested in Victor's research. Victor showed him his "Meth" lab and told him about his research on methanogens.

"You don't do sex research here do you doc?" asked Joe, as he was leaving.

"No." replied a puzzled Victor, "just methane research."

"LOCAL SCIENTIST USES SECRET SEX POTION TO SEDUCE WOMEN" read the headline in the next issue of the Brooklyn Raptor. The column added, "Dr. Victor Lebeau, a microbiologist at the University Hospital denies he is engaged in sex research but the Raptor has learned from sources who chose to remain anonymous, that recently numerous women have been drawn to him almost against their wills and have had brief sexual encounters with him. "I don't know how he does it," said one of his victims, "but I had to have sex with him. " He's not good looking or smart, or rich, or anything. He must have something up his sleeve."

Victor was aghast, but his disquietude was quickly interrupted by a phone call from Uncle Bert. "Your Aunt Trudy baked you a strudel. Lots of raisins and nuts," he announced. "She wants me to bring it over to you right away. And, by the way, nice going! Looks like you took my advice. Never thought you'd finally get indoctrinated. But you did it, big time. I'll be right over with the strudel."

Bert's visit was short. He dropped off the strudel, asked to use the bathroom, and left. Victor noted that on leaving, Bert smelled of cinnamon. When Victor looked in the bathroom, there was less after shave lotion in the bottle than before. Bert must have used some of it.

Chapter 14

The following day Victor answered the phone in his office. "This is Samantha Campbell" said the voice, "D & C is very interested in your research and I'd like to have a few moments of your time today to discuss the possibility of partnering with you. This could be very lucrative for you. Would you have a few minutes this afternoon to explore some possibilities?"

"Forgive me" answered Victor, "but what is D and C?"

"D and C," Samantha replied, "is Doctor & Campbell, a producer of personal care products and items used in almost every household in the U.S. I'm Executive Vice President of Business Development for our pharmaceuticals branch. I'd like to meet with you today but not at your work place. How about the cafeteria at the Brooklyn Museum? It's only a ten minute walk from the Hospital and we'll be pretty anonymous there."

That noon, Victor waited inside the lobby of the museum looking out at the fifteen foot high replica of the Statue of Liberty in front of the museum thinking "*Liberty was a bit plump*". A Jaguar convertible pulled up in front of the museum. The driver removed a wheel chair from the trunk and the passenger slid easily into the chair. She moved a joystick on the left arm rest and the motorized chair pulled forward. The driver waited outside smoking a cigarette before entering the building.

The woman wore a business suit. Her face was attractive but not animated. It looked to Victor as if it had been chiseled from marble. She wore no apparent make up. Her hair was brown and cropped short. Her legs were thin and did not move.

Samantha drove directly toward Victor, and smiled briefly. The smile was there for a second, almost like a twitch, and then was gone. Her driver stayed at a distance from them.

"Thank you for arranging your day to meet me here." She said. "Why don't we first walk around in the exhibits for a few minutes?"

The subjects of a late Nineteenth Century French impressionist painter's works seemed peaceful to Victor, mostly lakes, and boats and scene of city streets, not like the unease Victor felt about what Samantha Campbell might want from him.

Before her accident, Samantha had been the captain of the fencing club at Princeton, and after she graduated, she had worked for the CIA in counter-intelligence. Bruce, the driver of the Jaguar, had been a colleague at the CIA.

After her automobile accident three years ago, she decided to join the family business. The company had begun in the mid Nineteenth Century as a drug store started by her great grandfather "Doctor" John Campbell. At his death, it fell to her grandfather and then, at his death, to her father. "Dad" had taken the company public and had turned it into a huge presence in the business world. She had never before Victor, been asked "What is D & C?"

The museum cafeteria was small but pleasant. It was quiet on weekdays and they had no company near enough to hear them. Bruce sat several tables away but took a short cigarette break during Samantha's brief meeting with Victor.

"You can call me Sam. May I call you Victor?" Samantha scrutinized Victor. She had learned to use all of her faculties to quickly size up acquaintances and decide whether they were being truthful, and whether they were hostile. In Victor's case, she also had another motive. Victor seemed to be neither self assured nor particularly handsome, qualities she would have expected in a man who was uniquely successful with women. Yet, as she sat opposite him, she felt herself gazing at his chest, his shoulders, and his face with some pleasure. She could not deny that she was attracted to him and the longer she sat opposite him, the more attractive he appeared and the more she liked the idea of working with him, and of being with him.

Then, as she became more aware of these feelings, she realized that there must be some truth to the idea that this rather ordinary man must have something special to make him so attractive to women.

"Victor, I know you've had numerous sexual encounters recently and that this pattern is new for you. My colleagues have spoken with some of these women. I know that you also have a special friend with whom you seem very happy. I know where you work and I'm familiar with your project for the Department of the Energy. My reason for telling you all of this is not to make you uncomfortable. Just the opposite, I want you to know that you have nothing to fear from us and nothing to hide. We applaud your research and want nothing other than to partner with you, support your research, and hopefully, make you wealthier than you could ever have dreamed. We would also find a place in this venture for Polly if you want it. Is what I've said so far on track?"

"I guess there's no point in denying it. You and all the readers of the Brooklyn Raptor already believe it. But I'm not sure that I'm ready to confirm anything special right now."

"I understand your concerns, but you have to understand that such a product would have mass market appeal and would be of great interest to us. I need some help from you to begin working on an offer to you. I don't expect you to tell us much at this point but would you give me any hint of what may have given you any special attraction for women, something I can take to my Board"

"What can I tell you that will help?"

"You could start by telling us when you first noted this change and what you think may have produced it."

"I bought some new shaving lotion. It was a brand I never saw before. Within a day, women were coming on to me. I still have some of it left."

"That's a good start Victor. I'm sure we can do business. Hold onto that lotion. I'll be back to you shortly and we can talk more. My goal is to partner with you to identify, produce, test, and market the active ingredients that we discover together. If not, I can probably still make you a substantial offer just for the lotion."

Victor's heart was beating rapidly with excitement. "Can I think about this for a little while?" he asked.

Chapter 15

Victor appeared unexpected at Polly's door that evening. Her facial expression was not as angry as he had expected. By now she had surely learned of his dalliances with other women. She stood to one side to allow him to enter.

"Polly, I'm really sorry," he began. "I'll stop using the aftershave and the deodorant. I've tried to keep away from women as much as I can, and, I haven't slept with anyone since we were last together. I swear!"

"Victor, I was really annoyed at you until yesterday. But now that I found out what's really going on, I know you couldn't help yourself. The substance we found on your face **was** androstenol! And not only that, your armpit sample has tons of it."

Victor thought for a moment. He had been reading up on human pheromones and androstenol was one of the more likely ones. He replied "I know that androstenol has a musky odor and is sexually attractive to women. But it only lasts about 20 minutes on the skin before it's broken down to androstenone which smells like urine and is repellant to women. So, I ruled it out as the cause."

Polly reached out and touched his hand. "But not in your case. There was lots of androstenol and almost no androstenone. You were irresistible to women with an intact nose who were close enough to smell you. And how could a naïve soul like you have resisted? I believe you when you say you're done with all of that now and that you'll be faithful to me now. I trust you."

"You do? You believe me? You trust me? Well you can! I'd rather be with you than with anyone. Besides, it will be a lot less tiring." Then he asked "So I have really sexy armpits?"

"The sexiest armpits anywhere."

"Well how about you Polly, is that why you like me, for my pits?"

"I don't think so. I always had a crush on you. But you didn't turn me on at first. And now I know why. I have pollen allergies that make it hard for me to smell anything in springtime. By the fall, when my allergies lighten up, you'll be even more irresistible to me than you are now. I can't wait."

"So," said Victor, "I suppose it's my job to figure out why my androstenol doesn't turn into androstenone, right?"

"Right !" said Polly.

That evening Victor went to his lab and looked at the gloves that protruded into the anaerobic chamber. He saw that they had become frayed. He scraped with a sterile Q-tip, the inside of the gloves, the side that came in contact with his hands and wrists when he worked in the chamber. He touched the tip of the Q-tip to the surfaces of two Petri dishes. He placed one Petri dish in the anaerobic chamber and the other into an ordinary oxygen-containing incubator.

Chapter 16

Victor was firmly asked to attend a meeting with the dean of the medical school. The meeting was in the dean's office. He assumed that the meeting was about his sudden notoriety as revealed in the Raptor. The dean and the hospital director were seated on one side of the rectangular wooden table. His department chair and the university attorney, sat opposite them. Victor sat alone at one end.

The meeting was not about his peccadilloes and the embarrassment they presented to the Medical School. It was about his research. Victor informed them of D & C's interest in his work and their willingness to partner with him.

"You wanna what?" boomed the dean. It's not your work! The research belongs to the Medical School. You can't just peddle it to anyone you want. We're your primary employer. We own it."

"Just a moment," intoned the hospital director, "He does have an appointment at the medical school but the hospital pays most of his salary. And furthermore, he works in our space in the hospital labs, uses our electricity, our heating, our building. We're not going to neglect the hospital's interests here."

Victor's department chairman chimed in "Let's not forget that Vic was hired by me and is a faculty member of the Department of Pathology. We support him directly and indirectly."

The University lawyer added, "Not so fast. Each of you wants a piece of the pie from this maybe successful research project. May I remind you that the Department of Pathology, Medical School and the University Hospital are just branches of Empire State University? Forget about any deals until this issue goes to the University Board of Regents. And I'm not so sure they would approve this venture at all considering Dr. Lebeau's current notoriety. I can just see them imagining the next headline in the Brooklyn Raptor 'University approves deal for hospital lothario to debauch morals of unsuspecting women.'"

Victor's hopes of working with his suddenly fractious institution diminished with each of his boss's comments. "I don't want to make things even more complicated than they already are," he moaned, "but the grant that pays for this research is from The U.S Government. They may have some interest in keeping any of my work classified and they may decide that they own all of the results."

The attorney ended the meeting, "We're working on setting up a committee to enable joint ventures with private concerns regarding intellectual property developed at the University. The president is expected to decide on the composition of the committee in the next month or so. The committee should begin its first meeting in a few months and is scheduled to meet every three months to decide on which if any of the proposals to consider. There is already a backup of thirty six projects to think about. If you write up your plan for working with the private entity and how you expect it to benefit the University, I'll add it to the pile, but it may take a while before it's considered."

The attourney smiled and said "Chin up Victor. Don't look so glum. Meanwhile, please keep this meeting under your hat. And also, please keep (pointing) **that** in your pants."

Victor dialed Samantha's number "Hello Samantha, bad news over here. The University, the Medical school, and the Hospital have no way of working together on partnering and the U.S.

government still doesn't know about it. This mess may take years to settle."

Samantha laughed "Glad I'm in the private sector. Are you still working on your pheromone? It must be a pheromone."

"Yes, I think we're getting pretty close. I think we may already have a suspect growing in the lab. But I just don't know what we'll be able to do with it when we find out. But nobody has dibs on the aftershave lotion. I own that free and clear. Are you still interested in it? I had no sex until I started using it."

"I haven't been able to find anything like it anywhere and my people have been looking very hard. You bet I'd be interested!" answered Samantha.

Chapter 17

Polly and Victor alternated staying at each others' apartment. It was not only fun, it also was reassuring to Polly, who trusted Victor, mostly.

"Polly, I cultured the inside of the gloves of the anaerobic chambers," he announced, "That's where I put my hands and wrists every morning. It's just a few inches from there to my armpits. Each morning I may have been dosing my armpits with a culture of bacteria that could inhibit the conversion of androstenol to androstenone. That would explain why my pits were so seductive by the evening. Then in the morning, all was showered away for the new day."

He paused and thought for a moment. "And there's something interesting growing in the culture. I gave samples to the electron microscopy folks and the photos show an extensive system of membranes inside the cell characteristic of methane-oxidizing bacteria. These are bacteria that use methane for energy and some of these are capable of growing in an environment with Oxygen. Maybe these bacteria were taking advantage of the frayed surface of the gloves and the small amount of methane that may have leaked out of the chamber through the gloves. I haven't got it in pure culture yet. I'll have to subculture it. Then we can see if it makes an enzyme or other substance that inhibits the change from androstenol into androstenone. If it does, we could try to track down the substance and maybe do an analysis of this bacteria's DNA to find the genes for this inhibitor. That way the genes could be transferred to other bacteria which would be easier to culture and would produce enough inhibitor to market commercially."

Polly's heart was pounding. "*I love this nerd, my beautiful, smart nerd*" she thought.

Chapter 18

It was ten o'clock in the evening of the next day and the janitor had retired his Swiffer for the rest of his shift. His sat on one chair with his feet planted haphazardly on another. His head drooped and his breathing was slow and regular with an occasional snore. His keychain with lots of keys including the master key to the whole basement of the building rested on the floor. His Identification badge, labeled "Joe Penner, Custodian, Empire State Hospital," in its clear plastic case, hung from a loose plastic strap around his neck.

When he awoke two hours later, he didn't notice the absence of the passkey from the key chain or the ID badge from its holder.

The next day, when he arrived at work, he discovered them in his locker. Strange, he thought that they were there. He didn't remember putting them there.

The following day, Victor smelled smoke as he walked the short distance from the subway stop to the hospital. Two fire engines were leaving the scene and one of the entrances to the hospital was blocked off as was the staircase to the basement level nearest to his "Meth" lab. He took the other staircase and saw, when he got to his lab, that the inside of the lab was drenched and cluttered with burned furniture and a pile of scorched plastic and metal in place of the anaerobic chamber. Nothing recognizable remained of the cultures it had sheltered. On the floor was an anaerobe jar, the kind that was used to transfer anaerobic cultures from place to place without exposing them to oxygen. The lab had several of these, but they were slightly smaller and shaped differently from the one he now found in the lab. Although he could not get close due to the yellow tape barriers put up by the police, he was sure it was of a different brand.

And one more thing. There was a cigarette butt on the floor.

Chapter 19

Fortunately, Victor's data gathered from all of the previously studied methanogens were backed up on the University's information system's servers. But the lab was a mess and there was no way of recovering the current methanogen on which Victor was working or the methane-oxidizing bacteria that were the suspects for stabilizing the androstenol. These cultures, the gloves, and the chamber had all been burned up.

When Victor returned to his apartment that evening, two voicemail messages awaited his response. He called Samantha first. He told her that since the cultures had all been destroyed in the fire, the only hope was the aftershave lotion.

"You'd better come over with the lotion and we'll finish the deal," said Samantha, "Bruce had a little accident and is recovering in Switzerland. So for the moment, I have no driver."

"What was he doing in my lab last night?" asked Victor.

"I'm not saying he was or wasn't in your lab, but if he was, he certainly wasn't trying to blow it up!"

"Well," said Victor, "whoever it was, came equipped with an anaerobe jar which was still in the lab. I guess he didn't leave with the cultures he wanted."

"Maybe not," she said. "Maybe he or she had two containers and left with one of them with the cultures."

"Or else," said Victor, "he opened the airlock, tried to get out the cultures, and blew the place up when some of the hydrogen inside escaped."

"Hydrogen," she said, "I thought it was Methane inside the chamber. Methane is supposed to burn gently with a blue flame."

"It does, if there's a small amount of it. But in mines, it's present in greater concentration, is called coal gas, and has killed lots of miners when it exploded. But in this case, the small amount of Methane in the chamber was not nearly as important as the hydrogen. Hydrogen is explosive in as little as four percent in the air and was at five percent in the chamber, especially when it came in contact with you know who's cigarette. The butt was on the floor."

They agreed on a price for the remaining aftershave lotion. It was small change for D&C but a great deal to Victor.

The next day Victor and Polly met for lunch at the Brooklyn Botanical Garden. It was June twenty first and Victor had not been approached for sex by anyone but Polly in almost a month.

"How would you like to take a trip?" asked Victor.

"Where would you like to go? Asked Polly.

"I was thinking of Paris." Said Victor.

"Great! I'll start putting all of my small change in a pickle bottle and in a few years we'll have money for the airfare." Thought Polly.

Victor handed her two round trip tickets for Paris for the next week with an open date for return. Polly gasped.

"And I have something here for you from my mother," he said. "She gave this to me for you."

Victor held out a small jewelry box containing his mother's diamond ring. She had given it to Aunt Trudy to keep for Victor until he gave it someday, to his wife.

"How wonderful of her," said Polly," tears streaming down her face, "Are we getting married in Paris?"

"No" said Victor, "let's get married here. But my father called. He's single again. I thought we could go see him in Paris and give him the underarm deodorant."

CREATION

Celeste lowered her feet to the floor. It was nine thirty in the morning and there were sounds of people outside the ladies' room. She had been perched on the toilet seat cover since nine AM, when the palace was opened to the public. Her legs were cramped. She had been sitting on the toilet seat throughout most of the night and only got her feet off the floor to prevent them from being seen by the people who opened the building.

She opened the stall door and walked to the room where Bernini's Apollo stood. Apollo, in his robe and carrying a lyre, was the grandest sculpture in this, the former Ducal Place of the Malvecchios, once one of the richest and most often poisoned families in what is now Italy.

She noted the group of tourists standing in front of her Apollo. Their guide glanced at Apollo, yawned, gave the approximate date when it was made, and mentioned that Bernini also was one of the great architects of the Italian renaissance. The group moved on and Celeste could now see her work.

The sight of Apollo, even after the many times she had seen him, sketched him, and wondered at his beauty, still made her tremble.

Another group now stood in front of Apollo. The leader of this group, a tall lovely, red-haired woman, appeared to be a scholar followed by her disciples, rather than a tour guide. Celeste could hear her pointing out the natural folds of Apollo's garment, the fine anatomic details of Apolo's shoulders and thighs, and the grace with which he held the lyre, "just as if he were about to play it for his audience. It was "a work of art that could only have come from Bernini."

She stared at the statue and was silent for a moment, looked puzzled, and then whispered something to the person nearest her. The group moved on.

What had she seen? Was it Celeste's work? Had she noticed?

Other groups came and went. Nobody seemed to see what interested Celeste until a group of young girls accompanied by their teacher, arrived. One of the girls nudged another, pointed slyly at Apollo's groin, and they both tittered quietly. Celeste held her breath. The teacher made no comment and the group moved to a nearby mural.

Now Celeste was certain. At last, someone had noticed her work! It was worth it, hiding in the ladies room as the museum closed the night before, standing on the toilet cover so her legs would not be visible under the door of the stall, waiting until everyone was gone but the old watchman, and until he was soundly asleep.

Quietly, she removed from her purse, the marble penis that she had carefully carved. She filed the base gently and almost silently, so that it was an exact fit to the stump left by the madman who, centuries ago, had, in a fit of righteous zeal, hacked it off and shattered the pieces.

Her first lover, Mario, had unknowingly and unbeknownst to Celeste at the time, been the model for the part that she had made to complete this, the most perfect representation of male beauty that she had ever seen. She remembered her first time with Mario. Half rape, half submission, her mixed feelings of rage and joy, and her amazement at the change of his penis from what seemed enormous at first, to a small limp, thing, curved and unable to support its own weight. This nonthreatening penis is the one she carved for Apollo.

After her miscarriage, Mario had gone off to sea but she could sketch him from memory. Her sketches of him now lay in a large folder covered with many more recent sketches, some of more recent lovers. But none of the others could she sketch from memory.

Other visitors came, some seemingly enraptured by Apollo, some not wasting more than a moment or two with him. It seemed as if the women, and a few men, spent more time looking at Apollo than they would have before today, but maybe that was just her own view, imposed on them.

She went out for lunch, walked out in the palace gardens, and returned before closing. She found her perch on top of a toilet in the ladies room and again waited until she would not be disturbed. When everyone was gone, she again entered Apollo's room, stood before the statue, climbed up on the pedestal with him, and put her arms around his shoulders. Tears filled her eyes.

She reached into her purse, took out the smallest of chisels, and tapped it on the spot where the penis was glued to its base, watched her handiwork fall to the floor, and left.

The Icon of Saint Petersburg

The shop was in central St. Petersburg near several hotels frequented by foreign tourists. The icon was in the top shelf of a glass cabinet by the far wall, opposite the entrance. The view from his cabinet was a good one. He was propped up against the back of the cabinet and could see the patrons arrive and leave. When a woman bent over his shelf to better see him or the teapot to his left, he sometimes caught sight of a pleasant cleavage. It would have been enough to set his heart beating if he were not metal, and the size of a thin mobile phone. Today the light was just right, and in the morning sun he could see a partial reflection of his surface in the overhead glass pane of the cabinet. The reflection showed a low relief depiction of a man in a suit of armor, on horseback and carrying a spear. The spear was pointed at another man cowering on the ground.

An angel in the sky above them smiled down at the man on horseback.

"It's probably Saint Dimitri," he thought. "I'm supposed to be Saint Dimitri," he said aloud.

"You don't talk like a saint," said the teapot.

"Listen Tchainik," the icon replied, "And you don't whistle like a teapot."

"I don't whistle. Tea kettles whistle. I'm a teapot, and I'm on vacation in this cabinet. I can just sit here looking pretty. No whistling for me."

Two men looking like Americans entered the store. Their eyes searched the cabinets and the taller of the two walked quickly towards the icon.

The icon remembered the last time someone had showed interest in him. Ludmila, the owner had taken him from the cabinet, put him in the hands of the foreign tourist, and groaned, "This icon was taken from the bloody hand of the Tzarina right after her bullet riddled body crumpled to the ground. She clutched it so tightly, even in death, that she left a small dent in the corner over here. "She pointed to a small irregularity in the metal surface of the icon.

The tall man stared at the Icon, turned it over and looked at both surfaces, and said, "This should do it for Peter."

The shorter man looked over at the icon. "What's Peter going to do with it?" he asked.

"Peter's pretty religious. I said I'd bring him back an icon."

"Oh my God" thought the icon; "this guy is serious. Look at the way he's checking me out. Careful there! Don't cover my eyes."

The shorter American persisted, "He's religious. Does that mean he's going to pray to this thing?"

"I don't know," said the taller man, as he began to haggle over the price with Ludmila.

"He's going to buy me for some putz who's going to pray to me? He'll want miracles! I'm retired! I was never good at miracles. Once in a while I got lucky and something good happened and I got the credit. But how often is that going to happen?"

The tall man produced a small lead-lined protective bag once used for film and placed the icon over it in various directions to see how it would best fit. It was forbidden to take icons out of Russia and he would have to smuggle it out.

A small tear appeared at the end of the teapot's spout. She would miss the icon and his salty conversation. She watched as the icon went head first into the bag. She could barely hear his last muffled cries as the bag was closed about him, "Let me out of here! I don't want to work!" and finally, "I'm a knock off. I was made in China!"

JOURNEY

It was the first of July in 1934 and Maria lay in a hospital bed in Haute Savoie, in Eastern France. She raised her bruised hand to her pale face and moistened her lips with a wad of cotton she had dipped in a bowl of water.

"*Not a bad place to die.*" She thought. "*Quieter than Paris, but a little too dark in this room.*"

Her daughters, Irene and Eve, had already visited her this week and would not be back until next week. She slept much of the time. The rest of her waking hours, were filled with reminiscences of her work in Paris, her childhood in Warsaw, her two visits to Stockholm, and her dead husband Pierre.

Of what use now was her fame? Not much, for an old woman, alone most of the time with only her thoughts. She was now too weak to walk or to even sit long in a chair. She had no desire for food and could only drink sips of water.

Possibly out of respect for her former stature, her doctors had arranged for blood to be removed from her daughter Eve's arm, and then transfused into a vein in her arm. Transfusions were uncommon at that time.

Her body was no longer making enough red blood cells to prevent weakness, enough white blood cells to prevent infection, or platelets to keep her from bruising and bleeding. Eve could only give blood once a month which was not enough to make up for Maria's worsening anemia. Irene's blood could not be used because it was of a different type from hers. Maria wondered if her body had been poisoned by the specimens of Radium and Polonium that she often would carry on her person during much of her working life.

Three days after she stopped taking food and water, Maria drifted in and out of consciousness. Her nurses knew the end was near. Her doctors had discontinued her blood transfusions.

Then the door to her room opened and a man entered. The room was suddenly illuminated as the man's face became clear to her.

"Kasimir," she glowed as she spoke his name. "It's been a long time!"

"Yes," said the man, "Am I disturbing you?" he asked.

"Of course not!" She replied. "I never expected to see you again."

"I'm sorry," he said. "We were so young and my parents wouldn't hear of it."

"I waited for you." She said, "I always expected that we would be married in spite of your parents. But I couldn't wait forever. And then I met Pierre, also a physicist, like you and me. We had a good life until he was killed."

"Yes, I'm glad for you. But my parents are now long dead, we are getting on in years, and, Maria Sklodowska, I want to be with you for the rest of the time that we have remaining. Will you come back with me to Warsaw?"

"Oh Kasimir, I've been so weak! I don't know if I can even get out of this bed."

"Try my dear. Please try."

Maria pulled at the bed sheets and they were surprisingly light. She pulled them off with ease and put her feet on the floor. She summoned all of her strength to stand, and with the support of Kasimir, she felt stronger and walked with him to the door.

He picked her up and carried her out of the room, out of the hospital, and into his waiting Taxi. He placed her in a seat, sat beside her, and gently kissed her. She felt suddenly alive.

They drove to his hotel room and made love. The next morning they flew to Warsaw where she could see her mother, brothers and sisters waiting for her with arms outstretched.

"Not breathing." Said a nurse.

"No heartbeat." Said another.

"Strange," said the first nurse, she seemed so happy in her last moments.

ONE UP

The difference was that in the 2016 presidential election, candidates could no longer take campaign contributions from lobbyists, corporations, or industries. So their souls could not be sold to these interests but they were on their own raising campaign funds.

They could use the internet to generate small sums from large numbers of individuals but they also needed funds from wealthy people. So they still held one thousand dollars a plate fund raisers. Some used more creative methods to take maximum advantage of their celebrity, or personal attraction.

After the early primaries and caucuses the front runners for the Democatic Party's nomination for president were Walter Williams, the sixty five year old Senator from Louisiana, and Richard masters, the forty five year old Governor of the State of Vermont.

The older man was a veteran of three terms in the U. S. House of Representatives, including having served as chairman of the Ways and Means committee, and two terms in the Senate.

Masters, the younger man, had spent two years in the Peace Corp in Guinea. He then founded Upward Bound, an online minimum cost university with high school level and college level programs for youngsters who had dropped out of school. Upward

Bound became main stream in its second year and now furnished much of the course content of some inner city schools.

Masters' wife, Linda was in large part, responsible for the content of the high school courses and her attractive face was often seen giving the online lectures in science, her area of special interest. She continued to be active in the enterprise after her husband left to be governor.

Richard Masters was a riveting orator with great charisma. Linda was tall and athletic, a bit more understated than her husband but she was personable, thoughtful, and intelligent.

The couple was in their hotel room in Houston Texas, preparing for a one thousand dollars a plate campaign dinner. Linda had worked with her husband's staff to help tailor this speech to make it seem as if it had been written especially for this Houston audience.

She had finished dressing and was assisting her husband with his cuff links as he mused, "Williams just opened a can of hornets for himself."

"Worms" she corrected.

"He shouldn't have started this after dinner business. It'll be pretty tough for him," chortled Richard, "He'd better have a big stash of Viagra. He may have been buff twenty years ago but he's paunchy now. Won't be able to compete. I'll make twice what he makes at this game."

"Don't be so sure. It's been said that power is the greatest aphrodisiac and he has plenty of it. You'll need all the help you can get in this race."

She pushed his second cufflink in place and continued, "He's been around a long time and if he's going to take this path, he must have a pretty good idea of what he's doing. He probably has the women lined up and waiting."

"We'll see what they're willing to pay to sleep with that old man." said Richard, as he adjusted his dress jacket.

"You look stunning," she said as she put on her gloves.

"Thanks honey, I'll need to. For one hundred thousand dollars, this wealthy woman will want her 'next president of the United States' to perform well."

"You'll be just fine. Do you have a condom?"

"Of course!"

"Can you spare one for me? We could use another two hundred and fifty thousand dollars."

"Two hundred and fifty thousand dollars, from where?"

"From her husband."

"Oh."

Acknowledgements

Frank Scalia, Stephen Franklin, and Joseph Krieger, my oldest friends and friends to this day, helped to shape my mind with almost endless secular pilpul. The late Maurice B. Gordon gave me courage. My wife, Alida, gave me heart. My coworkers at M Labs, Deirdre Fidler, Sue Valliere, and Gene Napolitan, made it possible for us to get into the managed care business. My colleague Rodolfo Rasche and other colleagues at the University of Michigan, Department of Pathology to whom I showed tough cases, allowed me to sleep soundly at night and awake with ideas for this work. My colleagues at Joint Venture Hospital Laboratories, a Michigan network of hospital laboratories that contracts with HMOs, was the model for the Network in *Crime and Management*.

I am grateful to Melissa Brown for "Julio the cardinal," to Bob Elton, for his friendship and for his help with all things mechanical and some that are human.

Saulo Ribeiro and Phillip Zimbardo furnished insight into the philosophy of good and evil.

Holly Eliot, Paul Adler, Robert Kahn, Judy Gourdji, and Alida Silverman reviewed the manuscript at various stages and offered advice and encouragement.

I am grateful to Robert Killen, who rescued seven early chapters of the *Crime and Management* lost in a computer meltdown but retrieved from somewhere in its unconscious.

I am indebted to Sally Arteseros, Fritz Swanson, and Warren Williams, my editors who were each essential to the development and completion of the manuscript.

I am doubly grateful to Warren Williams whose insights into the characters and knowledge of aviation were of great help.

How Crime and Management Came to Be

The fictional operating systems of managed crime, as presented in this work, are analogous to those systems actually in place today in HMO managed healthcare plans in the U.S.A.

HMOs and Crime Management organizations would have three major principles in common:

1. Both involve insurance. HMOs insure against sickness and Crime Management Organizations (CMOs) would insure against crime.
2. Both are set up to prevent overuse of services, health care procedures for HMOs and criminal activity for CMOs.
3. Both reimburse providers of the services (Doctors, hospitals, etc. for HMOs, and a network of criminals for CMOs, on the basis of how many people are insured, rather on the number of services provided. In the case of HMOs, the system is designed to prevent unnecessary services: in the case of CMOs, almost all violent crime is to be prevented if the criminals are to make the most money.

Managed health care organizations (MCOs) have their equivalent managed crime organizations (MCOs) in this adventure. Members would need to enroll as individuals, through their employment, or through the federal Crimicare or State and Federal run Crimicaid insurance plans.

The federal agency that oversees payment for health care services, originally called the Health Care Financing

Administration (HCFA) and now called The Center for Medicare and Medicaid Services has its counterpart in the Managed Crime Financing Administration, (MCFA). Just as HMOs have an NCQA for tracking their quality, there is here an NCQA to assess crime control.

The University of Michigan, my employer at the time, became involved in two networks of hospital labs which now deliver the bulk of the outpatient lab services to the HMOs in the state. It was during the numerous long meetings needed to create these networks that the idea of Managed Crime occurred to me.

Could a network of criminals be formed to work together for their common good and that of the rest of us, and could such an unthinkable idea as Managed Crime actually work?

Disclaimer: This work is intended to be used only for entertainment. Social scientists who might take it seriously are warned that they do so at their own peril!

(Every book needs a disclaimer of some sort.)